# *The temptation to wake him was enormous*

Bess resisted. He was so beautiful. But, more than that, Luke's passion had been tempered with a gentle consideration and he had said thickly, making her feel special, "Luca. It is my birth name. To you I am Luca."

And now she asked herself if he had also invited Helen to use that name. The question slammed into her, a physical blow. The awful, inescapable, uncontainable shock of guilt.

She had spent the night with her sister's future husband. It was the ultimate betrayal, and she didn't know how she was going to live with herself.

Unless he had fallen in love with her as catastrophically as she had with him....

**DIANA HAMILTON** is a true romantic at heart and fell in love with her husband at first sight. They still live in the fairy-tale Tudor house where they raised their three children. Now the idyll is shared with eight rescued cats and a puppy. But despite an often chaotic life-style, ever since she learned to read and write Diana has had her nose in a book— either reading or writing one—and plans to go on doing just that for a very long time to come.

## Books by Diana Hamilton

HARLEQUIN PRESENTS
1588—SAVAGE OBSESSION
1641—THREAT FROM THE PAST
1690—LEGACY OF SHAME
1716—THE LAST ILLUSION
1732—SEPARATE ROOMS
1775—NEVER A BRIDE
1804—HOSTAGE OF PASSION
1841—SWEET SINNER
1858—WAITING GAME
1896—IN NAME ONLY

# DIANA HAMILTON

## A Guilty Affair

## Harlequin Books

TORONTO • NEW YORK • LONDON
AMSTERDAM • PARIS • SYDNEY • HAMBURG
STOCKHOLM • ATHENS • TOKYO • MILAN
MADRID • WARSAW • BUDAPEST • AUCKLAND

ISBN 0-373-11920-8

A GUILTY AFFAIR

First North American Publication 1997.

# CHAPTER ONE

THE way the dark stranger kept staring at her was completely and strangely disconcerting. There were times when Bess felt so uncomfortable that she didn't know where to put herself.

That too constant tarnished-silver gaze, sometimes oddly speculative, sometimes quite embarrassingly assessing, was making her a mixed-up mess of edginess, arousing a weird kind of insecurity that made her feel dismayingly like a turtle who'd lost its shell.

A shell-less turtle with a tummy bug, she amended as her stomach churned sickeningly around.

And she shouldn't be feeling like this—so hatefully and inescapably aware of a stranger—especially not at her own engagement party. She told herself that very firmly, adding that she wouldn't allow him to have any effect on her at all, and she was working up a comfortable mood of defiant control as Tom whispered in her ear, 'It's time we circulated, pet. There are dozens of late arrivals we haven't greeted yet.'

He was already releasing his hold on her and she went into a mild state of panic, clutching his shoulders, the ring he had put on her finger earlier glittering in the brilliantly lit, crowded room. 'Must we?'

She knew she sounded childish and the censor in her brain told her that her deep reluctance to leave the dance-floor, to mingle and inevitably be formally introduced to the dark stranger who had appeared as her sister's guest was totally irrational.

But knowing a fear was irrational didn't make it go away.

'Of course we must.' Tom's smile was wry as he unclamped her hands from his shoulders. 'We're public property tonight. No need to be shy.' But he didn't sound impatient; he never did with her.

She had known him for most of her twenty-four years and for all of that time he'd been protective of her, gently teasing her for what he liked to classify as shyness. So much so that she sometimes thought that even if she'd been the most extrovert soul on two legs he would have brainwashed her into believing she was the original shrinking violet!

But it wasn't as simple as that, as uncomplicated as being shy and retiring by nature. She had learned, early in life, never to thrust herself forward or try to muscle in on the limelight that had shone down on her sister all of her life. It simply didn't pay.

Two years older, the same age as Tom, Helen had always been the beautiful one, the witty one, the one who could charm and dazzle herself out of any scrape and into a position totally advantageous to herself, while Bess was the ordinary one, unnoticed when Helen was around, getting on with her life in her own quiet way, making no waves.

She exhaled on an unconscious sigh and Tom slid an arm around her tiny waist.

'Did I tell you how pretty you look tonight?'

Bess smiled at that. He sounded more dutiful than genuinely impressed. But then she decided that she did deserve the compliment, after all, because she had carefully dressed to please him.

When she'd chosen the understated beige silk dress to wear for their engagement party she'd known it would be exactly to his taste. He liked to see her looking neat and tidy, her curling copper hair tastefully subdued in a head-hugging pleat, only a token amount of make-up and nothing startling in the way of jewellery—just the simple gold chain he had given her at Christmas around her fragile neck.

He hated and distrusted flamboyance in any form. Which was probably why he had never approved of Helen, or her lifestyle.

And that, in turn, was why Helen's escort had been watching her almost from the moment she'd seen them arrive. He wouldn't be able to believe she was in any way related to the dazzlingly glamorous blonde creature at his side, she decided sickly.

But it wasn't important. It couldn't be. Wasn't she used to such reactions? Tom liked her just the way she was, and that was all that mattered, she told herself as she pinned on a smile and accepted the congratulations of those guests who'd arrived after she and Tom had taken to the dance-floor in the elegant conference-cum-hospitality suite of the area's most prestigious hotel.

'Some time within the next twelve months, but most probably this time next year. We've more or less decided on an Easter wedding. We have to find a suitable house first, of course—'

She was still smiling as Tom answered the inevitable questions about the wedding date, but her face froze as Helen bore down on them. The gold tissue she was wearing looked as if it had been painted on and the sheer dazzle of her smile would have put a firework display to shame.

'I'm glad you could make it,' Bess said dutifully, not at all sure whether she really meant it, and reluctant to look up at the tall, commanding figure at her sister's side because for some utterly insane reason he made her blood boil in her veins, firing her with a surge of adrenalin that was making her want to slap him!

And that wasn't like her at all!

Weeks ago, in a dismissive phone conversation, Helen had said that she didn't think she'd be able to make time to come home for the traditional family get-together at Easter. Modelling assignments kept her busy all over the world. Pity about the engagement party, she'd told Bess, but it couldn't be helped. She'd sounded bored.

'I wouldn't have missed it for a king's ransom— the first high spot in my baby sister's life!'

She wasn't bored now, Bess thought, stoically refusing to react to the unsubtle put-down. Helen was sparkling, the almost frenetic trill in her voice making Bess wonder if she'd been hitting the bottle.

But Helen didn't touch alcohol; she lived on bottled spring water, salads and fruit. She was careful about what she put into that fantastic body. That and her classically beautiful face were the only assets she had, so it was little wonder she looked after them so carefully.

Bess was shocked by her own descent into cattiness but swiftly exonerated herself when Helen moved closer to her silent escort, her body wriggling seductively beneath the gold tissue, her voice huskily amused now as she imparted, 'We've been waiting for ever for good old Tom to make an honest woman of her. They've been at it for years, can you believe? The parents all thought it was sweet but I used to shudder to think of what must have been going on behind the school bike sheds! Hilarious, isn't it, darling?'

'There has never been anything improper...' Tom began stuffily, and Bess felt her face go red with rare temper. For some extremely dubious reason she wanted the dark stranger to believe that she and Tom weren't as staid and boring as they looked.

But Tom had never liked Helen and his sense of humour was non-existent, so he wasn't about to let her comments go uncorrected, and Bess knew he was about to describe their chastity with cringe-making pomposity, when the stranger slotted in smoothly, 'It seems I must introduce myself. Luke Vaccari.' His voice was a dark, lazy drawl and it made all the tiny hairs on the nape of her neck stand on end. She felt, she thought dizzily, as if she'd been rubbed all over with rough hot velvet. 'Congratulations on your engagement, Clayton.'

Unwillingly mesmerised, she watched the strong, tanned hand clasp Tom's much paler, smoother fingers and savagely tussled with the clamouring instinct to slide away and hide. But she stood her ground. What did it matter if the stranger with the Italian-sounding surname was about to turn his attention to her? She had endured the dissection of his eyes all evening, so she could endure a few meaningless well wishes without going into a decline.

'You're a solicitor, Helen tells me.' He was still talking to Tom and Bess couldn't help looking at him more attentively. She surely didn't want to, but her eyes insisted on gluing themselves to his face.

Close to, he was far more incredibly good to look at than her earlier embarrassed and harried observations had prepared her for. Expertly cut, silky dark hair made the perfect foil for features that had been hewn with confidence and authority. He had an intelligent face, and it looked lived-in, too, which saved it from the banal unreality of complete perfection.

And his body, her waywardly devouring eyes informed her, was something else; tall, lean and lithe and packed with power. He looked, Bess thought on a wave of shock, like every woman's fantasy lover. His very being was a palpable assault on the senses.

'Tom's father is Daddy's partner—the firm's been around for a million years.' Helen couldn't bear to be left out of any conversation. 'So this has to be more a cosy merger than a wildly romantic marriage. Think it out: when the oldies are tottering around in Zimmer frames dear little Bess will have done her duty and produced the next generation of Braylington solicitors. I've tried to persuade her to stick her head above the parapet and find out what living's all about, but she simply won't listen.'

Which was an out-and-out lie, Bess thought, her soft lips compressing. Helen had never shown the slightest interest in her unremarkable kid sister. About to make her excuses and drag Tom back onto the dance-floor, she was paralysed by the rich velvet warmth of Vaccari's voice, pinned to the spot by the gleam of interest in those tarnished-silver eyes.

'So Bess is a homebody. There's nothing wrong with that.' An odd smile flickered at the corners of his wide, sensual mouth and then he addressed her directly, the hateful entrapment deepening until she was sure there were goose-bumps standing to attention all down her spine. 'From what I've seen of it, Braylington seems to be the archetypal English market town; I'm not surprised you prefer to stay put. I'm looking forward to seeing more of the area myself.'

'Actually, I live and work in London,' Bess managed to push out. She would not be patronised by him or anyone else. And she wasn't going to come clean and admit that her job as assistant to the manager of the South Kensington branch of a chain of travel agencies wasn't in the least bit glamorous or high-powered. So, before Helen could leap in and do it for her, she literally dragged Tom away.

Not that he needed much urging. He ran a finger round the inside of his shirt collar and muttered, 'How did she latch onto him? I don't know what they see in her. And he looks far too astute to be taken in by all that glitz.'

'Does it matter?' To be seen with Helen Ryland, supermodel, a man had to be a millionaire at the very least. Looks didn't mean a thing—or hadn't in the past, anyway. Helen went for the prestige of being seen with money—preferably old money— and the more of it the better. As well as no doubt possessing the mandatory millions, this new guy looked spectacular enough to take any woman's breath away, so no wonder she'd lowered herself to attend her kid sister's party. She had probably decided to upstage her.

Luke Vaccari was the first man-friend she'd ever introduced to her family.

And Bess wasn't the only one to have taken this on board, she discovered as her mother, still striking despite her fifty-odd years, bore down on them, closely followed by Barbara Clayton.

'Time to eat, you two. Barb reserved a table and the partners are filling plates at the buffet. I'd nab Helen and Luke too, but they're so wrapped up in each other it would be a pity to intrude.' She tucked her arm through Bess's and hauled her away in the direction of the room set aside for the buffet and bar while Barbara Clayton brushed imaginary lint from her son's dinner jacket, forcing him to lag behind, then promptly despatched him to help the two older men at the buffet.

Jessica Ryland lowered her voice and confided, 'If you and Tom had delayed your engagement a little while it could have been a double celebration.'

'It's serious, is it?'

Barbara's pale blue eyes, so like her son's, fastened intently on her old friend's complacent features and Jessica nodded.

'A mother knows these things. He's a wonderful catch. A highly respected financier, and although his father was Italian his mother was one of the Gloucestershire Dermots.' She leaned further over the white-covered table. 'Mother's instinct apart, just ask yourself when Helen has ever brought one of her man-friends home—let alone invited one to stay for a family long-weekend gathering!'

So that was what he'd meant when he'd said he was looking forward to seeing more of the area. Bess's heart plummeted to the soles of her feet. He made her uneasy just by being here tonight— spending the Easter break with him underfoot would be intolerable! And the thought of him married to Helen filled her with sudden, unreasonable panic.

'She's so lovely, she can have her pick,' Barbara was saying, the wistful note in her voice a reminder that, for a long time, Helen would have been the wife she would have hand-picked for her only son.

Wondering if her future mother-in-law still regretted her son's choice, Bess heard her own mother boast, 'She takes after me in looks, while little Bess here is an exact replica of her father.'

'I wondered why I have to shave twice a day,' Bess put in drily, not taking offence because she was used to put-downs and knew, in her mother's case, they weren't intentionally hurtful. Just thoughtless. Whereas in Helen's case...

Thankfully, the menfolk arrived with loaded plates, one of the white-coated waiters following with the obligatory champagne. Bess didn't think she could eat or drink a thing. For some crazy reason the whole evening seemed ruined.

Catching her troubled green eyes, Arnold Ryland asked, 'Enjoying yourself, Bessie?'

She nodded—what else could she do?—making herself smile as Tom slid into the seat beside her, and lied, 'Very much, Dad. You've done us proud.'

She would have much preferred a smaller gathering back at home, or best of all, a comfortable evening for two—just her and Tom quietly celebrating their engagement over a simple meal in a country pub. But her objections to this opulent thrash had been blithely dismissed. When her mother decided she knew best nothing could make her change course. Jessica Ryland sailed through life making everything go her way.

'Room for two more?' Helen's assertive, high-pitched voice made Bess flinch. She didn't know what was wrong with her this evening. She was used to her glamorous sister's need to be the centre of attention; she had lived with it all her life and it had never bothered her before.

But tonight things were different, and she didn't know why.

'Luke's finding me something to eat. The darling knows what I like.' Her slanting blue eyes swept round the table, not seeing anyone, simply lapping up the reaction to her golden presence, until Tom muttered, 'Two lettuce leaves and an inch of celery shouldn't tax him,' and then the fabulous lashes closed, the lancet glimmer between turning to frosty black ice, making Tom go red to the roots of his hair.

Bess muttered hastily, 'Let's go back and dance.' Anything to get away, stop the fight that was inevitable when those two spent more than half a second in each other's company.

And that suave, velvety voice said right behind her, 'It would be my pleasure.'

Bess froze, her heart thudding stupidly. She watched Vaccari's strong, elegantly boned hand place the tiny salad on a gold-rimmed china plate in front of Helen, saw her sister's brows peak with incredulity, and knew that unless Tom came to her rescue and claimed her there was no way she could get out of this.

But Tom had his head down, his face still flushed as he forked up cubes of lemon chicken. She could expect no help from that quarter, she thought wildly as Vaccari put a lean hand round her tiny waist and urged her to her feet.

There was an awful inevitability about all this, she thought numbly, her heart pounding so heavily that she felt light-headed. Helen's face was stony and Barbara Clayton said something to her son, but he huffed a low reply and continued eating and the partners were discussing golf handicaps—and Vaccari was sweeping her onto the dance-floor and there was nothing she could do about it.

The music was slow and smoochy, the lights dimmer now, the dance-floor empty apart from a couple who were wrapped together like cling film, most of the guests having taken off for the lavish refreshments, just a few of them still sitting at tables round the edge of the floor screened by the riot of hothouse flowers that proclaimed that when Jessica Ryland did something she did it in style.

His lean hand tightened around her waist and all at once, like the rush of a riptide, anger replaced that feeble compliance to the inevitable.

There was no law that said she had to do anything she didn't want to do. She hadn't wanted this ostentatious celebration but for her mother's sake she'd given in. But no one could make her dance with this man. It didn't make a whole lot of sense, but the thought of having him touch her, hold her against that elegantly clothed, painfully masculine body, made her feel frenzied.

'I don't want to dance,' she told him bluntly, her mouth mutinous, and he dipped his head slightly, his silvery eyes making a slow and deliberate appraisal of her features. His sensually crafted mouth barely moving, he told her, 'Of course you do,' and enfolded her within his strong arms, the sheer arrogance of his attitude making her stiff and unyielding. 'Relax. There's no need to be frightened.'

Frightened? The word hit her like a blow. 'I don't know what you're talking about,' she said rigidly. 'And I don't think you do either.' Instinctively, she bunched her fists and pushed them ineffectually against his chest, feeling the beginnings of panic now because the heat of his body was getting through to her, making her legs go weak. Her voice was croaky as she demanded, 'Why on earth should I be frightened?'

'You tell me.'

He was moving to the slow, seductive beat of the music, just slight body movements, but every sway and thrust of muscle and sinew and bone burned into her flesh.

The sensation was unbearable. Shocking.

She tried to move away but a dictatorial hand fastened on the lower region of her back, forcing her closer still, his head dipping down as he murmured against her ear, 'When a woman displays a mixture of antagonism and fear towards a lone male, there can only be one reason. Work it out for yourself.'

She shuddered uncontrollably. Work it out? It was so humiliating, she thought hysterically. He had picked up on the instinctive flashes of fear, of definite antagonism, and had come up with an answer she would never fathom.

And he wasn't a lone male. He was with Helen, part of a couple, and she couldn't think straight. Her brain was wallowing in fog because her body had unwittingly melted into his. They were close enough now to be one entity.

One of his hands slid to the back of her head. Her eyes languidly closed, and she felt the weight of her silky hair fall down to her shoulders as long, deft fingers removed the pins. And when he murmured, 'That's better. You have glorious hair, you shouldn't hide it,' she felt, just for a moment, an upsurge of unadulterated femininity; she almost felt abandoned, free...

Until she felt the heat of his mouth stroke the pulse-point at the base of her throat. She drew in a whimpering breath and opened hazy eyes on the dim and dreamy seclusion of a stand of potted palms—and the fear came surging back.

Fear of what he could make her feel. Something raw and primitive was calling from the depths of her being, singing out to him, to the man who was out of bounds for two very good reasons, and, on a choking gasp of panic, she opened her mouth on a defensive demand that they join the others.

Instead, however, she found herself welcoming the destruction of his lips as he ravaged her senses, sending her into a whirlpool of dark desires where nothing existed but the primitive beat of blood, pulses of sheer wickedness that burned out her brain, stripped her of every ounce of will-power, of decent behaviour, igniting her.

She had never dreamed that such sensations existed. How could she have known? Nothing about Tom's kisses had—

Sobbing with self-disgust, she found the strength to twist her head away.

'Don't! Oh, how could you?' Panic and shame roughened her voice, and she stared frenziedly into the silver gleam of his eyes and hated him.

His Italian genes would be responsible for his outrageous behaviour, she told herself, making him believe he could make it with any passable female under forty—even if he was a guest at her engagement party.

But what part of her was responsible for what *she* had done? She couldn't think about that. The thought of it twisted her brain into knots.

She was in agony as he whispered his reply. 'Easily. With great pleasure.' A dark and sinful smile played around the corners of his passionate mouth. 'And your response was...' One black brow drifted upwards consideringly as he chose his word carefully. 'Promising.' He touched her trembling mouth with a soothing finger. 'Put that fact together with the statement I made earlier and you might learn something to your advantage.'

Bess dragged in a sharp, painful breath. She didn't know what he was talking about. She didn't want to know what he was talking about.

Dragging her shaking fingers through the riot of her hair, hopelessly trying to restore some order, she walked away.

She would never forgive him. Never.

# CHAPTER TWO

'Now, you're sure you don't mind missing church?' Jessica Ryland asked as she pulled on her gloves.

Bess stated, 'No, I don't mind staying to see to lunch.' Which was what this was about, after all. 'Tom will be here straight after the service, so you and Dad can have sherry with the vicar and discuss your committee work with a clear conscience.'

'Sweet of you, darling.' Jessica straightened her hat in front of the hall mirror as her husband sounded the car horn outside. 'Don't let Helen sleep too late. Her eyes get puffy when she does. She wouldn't thank you for that, not with that lovely man of hers around.'

Bess didn't want to be reminded. She still felt bewildered and desperately guilty over what had happened last night.

According to her mother, Vaccari had gone walking. Bess hoped he'd disappear into a hole in the ground.

As soon as the heavy front door closed behind Jessica, Bess thrust all thoughts of Helen's man out of her head, went into the airy sitting room and lit the fire. Although the Old Rectory was centrally heated the early spring day was chilly, and a real fire was always cheerful. When Tom arrived they could have coffee in here and discuss her new job opportunity in comfort and peace.

She had meant to tell him about it last night. But when she'd returned after her encounter with the disgraceful Italian he and Helen had been having one of their vitriolic spats. They'd both looked as if they could slaughter each other.

The way she must have been looking, with burning cheeks and her hair all over the place, must have been the final straw, because Tom hadn't exchanged more than half a dozen words with her during the remainder of the evening, and every last one of them had been grumpy.

Watching the fire take hold, she heaved an exasperated sigh. She and Tom never fell out; everyone said how compatible they were. But he had seen the Italian sweep her onto the dance-floor; he had seen how she'd looked when she'd eventually returned. Had he guessed what had been happening? If he could have seen the way she'd responded to that devil's kiss he would have been disgusted. Ashamed of her. And she wouldn't have blamed him.

Thoroughly ashamed of herself, and not quite knowing how it had happened, she went to the kitchen. Lunch for six. Roast beef and all the trimmings with apple pie to follow. A suitable penance, she reflected as she covered her serviceable grey skirt and neat cream blouse with one of Jessica's aprons, since cooking was one of her least favourite occupations.

Half an hour later, making pastry, she could happily have hurled the rolling pin at Luke Vaccari's head when he sauntered through the door. Instead, she controlled herself and said in tones of deceptive docility, 'Helen's not up yet. Why don't you go and wake her?'

She wasn't going to stoop to her sister's level and bring up the subject of puffy eyes. And if he did as she'd suggested he'd be doing everyone a favour. He was looking throat-clenchingly virile this morning, in a soft black sweatshirt topping wickedly tight-fitting stone-coloured jeans. So Helen would welcome him into her bedroom with open arms. And his subsequent absence would mean that she and Tom could mend fences in peace and discuss her job offer.

'Let her sleep. She works hard enough.' Annoyingly, he refused the bait. He took a slice of prepared apple and crunched it between perfect white teeth. 'Something smells good. Beef? Is this what you're best at—finding your way to a man's heart through his stomach? Is this how you snared Tom?'

He'd said it as if she were incapable of finding a man any other way. And the derisory gleam in his eyes as they wandered over her small, neat person was a back-up statement if ever she'd seen one.

She slapped the pastry topping over the apples and trimmed it with rough, savage sweeps of the knife, a betraying flare of colour on her face as she snapped out, 'Did no one ever teach you manners? If you're as rude to Helen as you are to me it's a wonder she lets you anywhere near her!'

'I thought the dulcet tones were a put-on.' His smile was all sinister satisfaction. 'The antagonism's still all there.' He moved closer. 'What about the fear?' And closer still, until she was backed against the table, her eyes spitting green fire. His face was all menacing hard lines until he suddenly smiled. 'It's there. No need to repeat last night's lesson.' And then his tone altered, became gentler, softer. 'I behave impeccable around Helen. She doesn't need a bomb under her. But you do.'

Bess didn't know what he meant. He talked in riddles and she wouldn't give him the satisfaction of asking for answers.

All she wanted was for him to go away. She hated it when he was in the same room, hated it more when he was this close.

She had no way of understanding the untypical violence of her reaction to him but she did know that he robbed her of self-control. He had a shattering effect on her, and before she fully knew what she was doing she was pummelling his chest with floury hands, her head spinning as she ground out, 'Just leave me alone—you're insufferable!'

'Yes, I know.' He captured both her hands, making no real effort, his lazy eyes laughing into hers as he perched on the edge of the table, drawing her between his parted thighs. 'Fun, isn't it?'

*Fun*? Being forcefully held in such a wickedly intimate position was not her idea of fun. Frustration glared from her eyes as he disregarded her squirming efforts to pull away, his mouth curling with silky amusement as he chided, 'You haven't felt this fired up for years. If ever. Admit it. Be honest for once; say what you feel, not what you think other people expect you to feel.'

'I don't know what you're talking about,' she denied, regretting her inability to iron the quaver out of her voice. 'Why don't you back off and leave me alone? You're Helen's guest, not mine. I don't know what you're trying to do—what you want,' she finished desperately.

'I don't want anything I'm not entitled to try to take,' he countered enigmatically, his hard thighs tightening on either side of her taut, slender body. 'I'd be doing you a favour if I forgot my manners and took before I was offered.'

Heat was building up inside her. She couldn't cope with it. Or him. And if Tom were to walk in now—or Helen—what would they think, seeing them like this?

Panic and guilt pushed her heart up into her throat and forced out a frenzied whimper, and he slid his hands behind her shoulderblades, the pressure inescapable as he pulled her body into his.

'Relax, Bess.' His voice was unforgivably soothing, the touch of his hands, the imprisoning, sexy strength of his thighs making her unthinkingly respond to his gentling command as easily as if he'd touched a control button. 'I'm trying to open your eyes a little, that's all. I'm not aiming to hurt you, ravage you on the kitchen floor. Because, so far as any of us know, we only have one life to live. I hate waste, and you're wasting yours.'

'You know nothing about me,' she objected, and wondered why her voice was so submissive, why her head was burrowing into the drugging warmth of his impressive shoulders, why the thought of Tom's imminent arrival meant nothing to her now.

And she felt her entire body lose every scrap of resistance as his lean hand cradled her head as if he liked the way it felt against his body, and he contradicted softly, 'I knew all about you before I saw you. More from what Helen left out than from what she said. She's a beautiful, vital woman and as far as she's concerned you're not merely her pale shadow, you barely exist. And she's made sure that's the way everyone else sees you too. Am I right?'

Bess didn't answer. She couldn't. He had made her mind spin off into orbit. This wonderful, shocking intimacy had blanked out her brain, leaving only sensation.

'It's a criminal waste,' he continued in the same husky, hypnotic voice, as if he had expected no reply, not even the smallest effort at self-defence. 'You have far more potential than you realise, or have been allowed to realise. Tom's a nice enough guy, but he's not for you. You deserve more than the safe predictability of life with him. Go out and look for what you've never had. Break away—find the passion and drama of living—find yourself.'

The sudden surge of emotion that stormed through her was too intense to be borne and she pushed herself backwards within the confines of his arms. They were both mad. He for spouting such nonsense, she for listening—even for a second. He knew nothing about her; why should he say such things?

'Let me go,' she commanded tightly, her face going white when she saw his taunting smile.

The colour flooded shamefully back when he countered, 'You wanted it. When a woman uses physical force on a man she usually expects a physical response.' His arms dragged her back into the curve of his body. 'You asked for this, and you got it. So stop complaining.' The wicked gleam of his eyes was hidden by the sweep of dark lashes.

'Or isn't this enough? Are you asking for more? Is that what you're trying to tell me? Don't be afraid to admit what you feel.'

'No!' Appalled, she pushed the denial out, and to her shame felt her eyes swim with tears of humiliation and shame. Had he been right? It didn't bear thinking about, but she had never used her fists on anyone before. Had she unconsciously sought physical contact, using the small violence of her fists to provoke a response, taking it for granted that he wouldn't punch her right back but use a far more devastatingly effective method of responding?

She shook her head to clear it of the awful self-knowledge and the tears brimmed and fell. And that was her salvation, because he put her gently aside, brushing the floury deposits from his shirt, his voice blank as he said, 'I'll make coffee. We could both use a cup.'

Bess scrubbed her wet eyes with her apron, too emotionally distraught to say a thing, and turned to the sink, trying to block out the rattle of china, the chink of a teaspoon, to shut down all her senses as far as he was concerned because she didn't want to know what he was doing. She didn't want to know he existed at all.

She shot out of the way as he came to her side to fill the kettle—right over to the other end of the room—just as Tom came through the door, rubbing his hands and wrinkling his nose appreciatively.

'Jessica said you'd offered to make lunch. Smells good.'

His smile was so safe, so uncomplicated. Bess could have hugged him. But she wouldn't display any emotion in front of Vaccari. She'd done too much of that already—to her everlasting bewilderment and shame. Instead, she said quickly, 'You've timed it right. We're just about to take a coffee-break.' Which hadn't been the right way to put it, she decided wearily as Tom's face turned sullen, his eyes narrowing with suspicion as he watched the elegantly casual Italian take down an extra cup and saucer from the dresser.

'Break from what?'

Bess swallowed a sigh. Tom would be remembering her hectic appearance after she'd danced with Vaccari last night. She could have said, He's been manhandling me again. Do something about it. But she said no such thing. She knew, no matter how unjust it was, that the Italian would regard whatever outraged ferocity Tom was able to dredge up with no more trepidation than he would a bluebottle buzzing inside an upturned jar.

So she forced a smile, removing her apron as she walked over to the dresser.

'A break from cooking. Luke's just come in from a walk.' She felt sneaky, and vilely guilty. Vaccari would know now that she was capable of lying to her fiancé, if only by omission. She took another cup from the dresser. 'Take coffee up to Helen, would you?' she asked the enigmatically smiling brute. 'Tom and I will have ours in the sitting room.'

Thank heaven she sounded cool enough. And if her face was flushed then Tom would put it down to the heat of the kitchen.

But her attempt at appeasement hadn't worked, she realised as Tom followed her through with the tray of coffee. He sounded peevish as he muttered, 'Having Vaccari around is spoiling the whole weekend. I can't think why your mother invited him to stay.' He slumped down on the sofa, accepting the cup Bess handed him, stirring it irritably.

'She didn't. Helen brought him, remember? He's her latest,' she stressed. 'Everyone thinks it's serious because she's never introduced one of her menfriends before.' Colour touched her cheeks. She knew exactly why she'd made a point of mentioning that—forcefully reminding herself that Vaccari was Helen's man. Though she shouldn't need the emphasis, should she? She was happily engaged to Tom.

She made an impatient gesture with her hands, brushing the subject aside. She wanted to spend this time discussing her job offer. And for that she needed Tom in receptive mood, and enough time at their disposal to go into the pros and cons very thoroughly.

But the reminder that it had been Helen who had foisted the Italian on them seemed to have added to his displeasure. Bess couldn't understand it. On the surface, Vaccari was pleasant enough. Tom couldn't know what he'd said and done to her. And he couldn't possibly care who Helen got serious about. He couldn't stand her.

'What were you thinking of, sending him to wake her?' Tom grumbled, his face going red. 'It's like giving him an invitation to—well—' He went redder. 'It's hardly proper.' He lifted his cup and gulped at his coffee, as if he needed something to hide behind. Bess swallowed a smile.

Proper! He didn't know how unintentionally funny he could be. He would hate it if he thought she was laughing at him. But his old-fashioned attitudes, his rock-like steadiness, were the attributes which had drawn her to him. He was comfortable, safe and utterly reliable.

'Does it matter?' She perched on the sofa, close to him. 'Helen can take care of herself.' The thought that taking care of herself would be the last thing on her sister's mind right now made her breath snag in her throat and something painful claw at her midriff.

Hating her stupid reaction, she twisted her hands together in her lap, wondering why everything seemed to be going so wrong, and shook her head despairingly when Tom muttered dourly, 'I just bet she can.'

'I wish you could find some good in her,' she sighed. Helen had her faults, but she had her good points too. But Tom would go to his grave believing that everything about her was suspect. 'She's my sister, after all. Family. And if you're going to be at each other's throats every time you meet it won't be very comfortable for the rest of us.'

For a moment she thought he wouldn't answer, but when he took her hand and squeezed it, making her ring dig painfully into her finger, she guessed it was an apology and suggested, 'Let's go for a walk after lunch. Just the two of us. There's something I need to discuss with you.' And there wasn't time now, she realised. Not if she had to have lunch ready by the time her parents returned.

'And that is?' He carried his cup over to refill it from the coffee-pot on the tray and Bess wondered why he was distancing himself from her. He had never been demonstrative, yet on the all too rare occasions when they'd been alone together he'd always taken the opportunity to cuddle her, his tender kisses making her feel that she counted, was secure.

Could it possibly be that now they were officially engaged he had decided he had no more need to bother with physical assurances of his love and caring? She knew he wasn't highly sexed, but—

Swallowing an unhelpful spurt of anger, she explained mildly, 'I've had the offer of another job. It would be exciting and challenging, but there would be disadvantages. There's not time to discuss it now, not with lunch to see to. That's why I suggested a walk. I'm going back to town tomorrow afternoon and I have to give an answer on Tuesday.'

'You have a job,' he pointed out unnecessarily. He took his cup and stood with his back to the fire. 'It isn't as if you have a career, as such. You won't be working at all once we have a family. Why bother to change, especially if there are disadvantages? Why put yourself through the hassle of having to adapt to a new employer?'

'I won't have to adapt—' She bit off her explanation and stood up. She'd known she would have to discuss every detail, pick the subject over endlessly before he would feel able to give a considered opinion. But he appeared to be discounting it entirely without hearing the full story, and she hadn't known he could be like that.

Moreover, he was looking at her as if he disliked her, and she didn't understand what was happening. This should have been such a happy weekend but it had turned topsy-turvy, like a bad dream.

She began to stalk out of the room. She really couldn't bring herself to continue the discussion. She didn't want to have to talk to him at all. And that horrified her so much that she turned back, dismayed.

'Let's talk it through this afternoon. You haven't heard the details.'

She hadn't meant to sound antagonistic but hadn't been able to keep the edge out of her voice, and Tom snapped back, 'I don't need to. You're settled where you are, so why change things? It's not as if—'

'I'm a high-flyer,' she inserted crossly. Part of her brain was seething because he'd written the subject off, as if he couldn't be bothered to summon an interest. The other part was amazed that they were having their first quarrel.

'One career woman in the family's one too many. And no, you're not a high-flyer, thank the Lord. Stick with what you know, and just be yourself. That's good enough for me.'

Bess sucked in a painful breath. She felt as if he'd slapped her face. And she felt even worse—mortified—when Vaccari's cool drawl sliced through the heated, ragged atmosphere.

'Squabbling, my children? We can't have that, can we?' His silver eyes mocked her as he sauntered across the room, dropping with boneless grace onto the sofa, long legs stretched out in front of him as he purred, looking deeply, devastatingly, into her wide green eyes, 'Anything I can do to make things better?'

# CHAPTER THREE

'I SUPPOSE he thought he was being funny,' Tom muttered, following Bess out to the kitchen.

'I suppose so,' she shrugged, tight-lipped. She hadn't bothered to dignify Vaccari's remark by making a reply. She'd be a much happier woman if she knew she would never have to speak to him again.

Then, swept by a wave of contrition, she turned and wound her arms around Tom's waist. 'I'm sorry I was snappy.'

'Me too.' His arms enfolded her briefly. 'There's a funny atmosphere this weekend; it's getting to both of us.'

He dropped a kiss on the top of her head and Bess thought, We both know who's to blame for that, don't we? and held onto him with quiet desperation until he untangled her arms and offered placatingly, 'Tell me about your job offer after lunch. But I warn you, I don't think you should give it any real consideration—'

'Fine, we'll just talk about it.' Miffed, Bess swung briskly away, cutting him off before he could repeat his opinion that she was not, and never would be, high-flyer material.

He was probably right, and she shouldn't feel hurt because he'd voiced his opinion. This time yesterday she would have agreed with him and possibly even felt a little bit smug about being the sensible sort of woman who knew her limitations and was perfectly content with what she had.

So why was she feeling hurt and undervalued for no reason? No good reason, she amended swiftly, pushing the things Vaccari had said to the bottom of her mind. She couldn't imagine why. And wasn't even going to try to work it out.

She became quite cynical when, over lunch, Helen said with sugary surprise, 'This is perfectly cooked. Well done, little sister. You should have woken me; I could have helped. This is supposed to be your weekend—and Tom's, of course.'

She was toying with a small slice of beef and looking spectacularly golden in a daffodil-yellow sweater, and her belated offer of help had to be for the Italian's benefit. Any reply Bess might have made was swamped by Jessica's, 'Bess needs the practice. Twelve months from now she'll have to give Tom three good meals a day. And you need your rest. You told me how tiring your assignment in the Bahamas was—you have to look after yourself. Don't you agree, Luke?'

'How awful for you.' Bess didn't want to hear gooey, solicitous sentiments from Vaccari, especially not if they were directed at her got-it-all sister. She helped herself to another roast potato. 'Personally, I'd love the opportunity to tire myself out in the Bahamas.'

And, so saying, she effectively silenced the lot of them.

The afternoon walk with Tom hadn't been a success either, Bess ruminated as she drove herself back to London on Bank Holiday Monday afternoon.

As soon as they'd set out she'd explained it all. How Mark Jenson, her former boss at the agency, had set up on his own six months ago, renting elegant premises in Knightsbridge, working hard to establish the kind of travel agency that specialised in holidays for the discerning, seriously wealthy traveller.

'He's offering off-the-beaten-track unadulterated luxury to people who are willing to pay top whack to be pampered,' she'd explained. 'It's really taking off, and now he needs an assistant to seek out and vet new venues in the more exotic parts of the world to make sure everything meets his high standards. And do you know what? He thought of me! The job's mine if I want it, but he needs to know by Tuesday.' Her face had lit up. A little squirm of excitement had built up inside her. It was there whenever she thought about the offer.

But she'd said honestly, 'The only downside is the newness of the venture. He's got more prospective clients than suitable places to send them— so he needs new venues and more employees. But to get them he needs more capital, and if he can't get it the agency will stagnate and probably sink.' She'd tucked her arm through Tom's and reassured him happily, 'But he's a fighter. He'll raise the capital somehow.'

'You must be mad.' He'd walked steadily on, staring straight ahead. 'You're secure where you are. Where will you be if you join him and the whole thing fails? Because fail it will. You'll be unemployed. Safe jobs aren't easy to come by. We've decided you'll work for two years after we're married. Or had you forgotten? We've agreed to invest your earnings to create a nest egg before we start trying for a family.'

He'd given her a scathing look, shaken her hand from his arm and turned to go back to the house. 'You can't seriously consider jeopardising your chance to contribute to our future comfort and security? In any case, from the job description, you'd have to be out of the country looking for places to send people who probably wouldn't want to go there anyway. We'd see even less of each other than we do now.'

She'd had the definite impression that this last had been a complete afterthought. That the investment nest egg was of far greater importance.

Still aggrieved, she parked her car outside Brenda Mayhew's terraced house in Battersea, reached her luggage from the back seat and rummaged in her handbag for the doorkey.

If he'd said, Go ahead and take the job if you want to try your wings, but I'll hate having to see even less of you than I do now, she wouldn't have given Mark's job offer another thought. As things stood, though, she had the strongest urge to phone him right now and ask when she could start!

Sighing over her contrariness, she unlocked the door and walked inside. Brenda shot out of her sitting room, all middle-aged, grey disapproval, and stated the obvious.

'Oh, it's you. I didn't expect you back yet. You'll have to go out for supper. Wasn't expecting you; I haven't catered.'

'Don't worry about it.' Supper each Monday was fish fingers and mash. Bess wouldn't pine over missing it. And not for the first time she regretted having agreed to board here during the week.

When she'd first announced her intention of looking for a bedsit in the sprawling suburbs of the capital to avoid the daily drive into work and back, Barbara Clayton had come up with the perfect solution.

A local woman, Brenda Brown, as was, had been her domestic help until she'd married and moved to Battersea. They'd kept in touch—just a short letter tucked in with a card each Christmas. And it was just as well, Barbara had declared, because since she'd been widowed Brenda had taken in a lodger from time to time to help make ends meet. It would be ideal for Bess—a sort of home from home, someone to keep an eye on her, look after her...

Home from home it wasn't. But Bess hadn't felt uncomfortable enough to move out. She wouldn't find anywhere cheaper, and if the suppers Brenda provided were unusually dreary at least she was saved the chore of having to cook for herself.

She lifted her case and began to walk up to her dismal room, and Brenda called, making it sound like an accusation, 'A Nicola something or other phoned. If you call her back, work out the cost and leave the money on the table. And don't leave it too late. You know I don't like being disturbed after I've settled down to watch telly.'

Bess knew the older woman hated to miss a moment of her evening's viewing. She'd paid her licence fee and meant to get her money's worth. And when Bess used the phone she couldn't resist turning down the sound, ungluing her eyes from the moving images and applying her ear to the opened door...

Smiling wryly, Bess carried on up, looking forward to talking to Nicola. They'd been at school together before Niccy's father had made his millions and spirited his adored only child away to some select boarding-school. But they'd kept in contact—closer contact since Niccy had been promoted to assistant producer on one of the more popular TV soaps and her father, in celebration, had bought her a long lease on a sumptuous apartment near Belgrave Square which she currently shared with a chronically out-of-work actress with the improbable name of Dearie.

A nice long natter with her friend would help to cheer her up, she decided, tossing her case onto the narrow bed. She hated this new and unexpected feeling of being at odds with herself and Tom. It was as if the official engagement had unleashed a pack of demons neither of them had known were there, lurking in the background, waiting to pounce.

On her way back downstairs, she wondered if Helen and Vaccari had left Braylington yet. They'd been closeted with her father all morning—with her mother bustling in and out—and when they'd emerged for lunch Helen had looked radiant. She had no idea what the Italian's expression had been. She hadn't looked at him.

Annoyed with herself, she caught the thought and buried it deeply. He had no place in her head. Dialling her friend's number, she heard the sitting-room door creak open. She ground her teeth, swung round and said coolly, 'I'm timing the call, Brenda. You needn't trouble to check. I don't cheat.' And she sucked her lower lip between her teeth as the door closed again with a thunderous clunk.

She had never voiced her annoyance over the lack of this particular privacy before, enduring it grimly because her phone conversations were always innocuous. She didn't know what had come over her. And put it out of her mind as she heard Niccy's voice.

'Well, was it all wonderful—the engagement party? What did you wear? What's the ring like?'

Her spirits lifted immediately. Niccy was fun. And because she didn't want to sound like a misery she refused to say that the weekend had been far from wonderful, that her dress had looked dowdy against Helen's glitter, that her sister had produced a fantastic man who had made her think and do things that were totally alien. So she concentrated on the ring.

'A diamond cluster,' she said, automatically holding out her left hand. But the ring wasn't there and she went cold all over. Had she lost it already? Oh, how could she have done? Tom would be livid! Then she went limp with relief because she remembered now that she'd put it on the drainer when washing up after lunch. Jessica would find it and keep it safe. She would phone her later, just to make sure.

'And?' Niccy prompted. 'A central stone?'

'Just a cluster,' Bess answered quickly, recovering from the shock of thinking she'd lost it and squashing the disloyal thought that the diamonds were few and very tiny. Tom wasn't mean, she reminded herself. He simply disliked ostentation in any form—witness his disapproval of Helen. How often had he scathingly said that she looked like a Christmas tree with all the lights switched on?

'Really?' Niccy snorted. 'If I'd been Tom I'd have given you a whacking great emerald to match your eyes! Some men don't have a clue, do they? Listen, you must stop hiding him out in the sticks; get him up to town one of these weekends. We could have fun. I'll have to meet him some time, won't I?

'And talking of fun—which is why I called you in the first place—Dearie's moving out. She's met this guy—fabulous to look at, all teeth, muscles and long blond hair. But he obviously keeps his brains in his pants—it will all end in tears, I told her. But she's besotted—won't listen. The point of this being, will you move in?'

Bess's fingers tightened round the receiver. It was very tempting. Niccy's huge apartment was sumptuous yet homely, the atmosphere wonderfully relaxing. But...

'Thanks for offering, but I couldn't afford it. I'm saving to get married, remember. Sorry.'

She *was* sorry, too. The apartment, never mind being a world away from Brenda Mayhew's linoleum-covered floors and ugly furniture, was so much nearer her workplace and, far more importantly, Niccy was so much nicer to be around than her present landlady.

'Of course you could afford it,' her friend argued lightly. 'Peanuts. Just half-shares of the service bills. I like company—Daddy knows that; he doesn't expect me to ask my friends for rent money. If Dearie could find her share of the bills on her meagre income, you could! Think about it. Promise?'

'Yes. Promise.' The only thing stopping her jumping at the opportunity there and then was the certain knowledge that Tom would disapprove. He liked to think that Brenda was looking after her and had once said, only half-jokingly, she now suspected, that her landlady would soon let his mother know if she was leading a double life—kicking over the traces while she was out of his sight.

Ending the conversation after a few more minutes of light-hearted chat, Bess went up to fetch her purse to pay for the call, plus the one she intended to put through to check on her ring. But, the ring forgotten, she found herself sitting on the hard narrow bed pondering Niccy's offer.

Tom didn't own her. He couldn't dictate where she should live during the week. He was happy enough while she was under Brenda's watchful eye, but she knew he would feel uneasy if she moved in with the bubbly, fun-loving Niccy because she, Bess, might find herself having a wonderful time. Without him.

So she couldn't decide if moving in with her friend for the next twelve months would be worth all the aggro. And it was strange, she thought, her teeth worrying at her lower lip, how Tom and Vaccari had both told her to be herself. Yet their concepts of that were wildly different.

'Just be yourself,' Tom had said. 'That's good enough for me.' Thrifty and sensible Bess, thankful for what she had and was, making no waves, never yearning for the impossible or trying to make it happen. Excellent, dutiful, undemanding type wife material.

Vaccari had put it differently, telling her to break away, find herself, realise her full potential. In other words, forget Tom.

She made a sad little snuffling sound, feeling miserable. She had been so contented until this weekend—settled in her job, enduring her weekday lodgings because they weren't worth making a fuss about, looking forward to her future with Tom. She asked herself why things had changed and angrily pushed away the thought that Vaccari had a lot to do with it.

Utter nonsense. For some reason the wretch got his kicks out of tormenting ordinary, decent people. Throwing a spanner in the works was probably his idea of a fun thing to do. She could safely dismiss him and his troublemaking taunts from her mind. She would pretend he didn't exist. And if and when he ever married Helen, well, she'd—well, cope with having him as an in-law somehow.

What she had to do was examine her relationship with Tom, reinforce it in her mind, concentrate on his good points, forget the silly pique his remark about her not being high-flyer material had conjured up and get back to being sensible and reasonable again.

And she would never again give Vaccari room in her head.

But that wasn't going to be easy.

An irritated rapping on the bedroom door heralded her landlady's formidable presence.

'There's someone to see you. He's waiting downstairs. See what he wants and get rid of him. You know I said no visitors unless by arrangement. Answering doors and running up and down stairs isn't my idea of a peaceful evening.'

Waiting downstairs he wasn't. When Bess saw the Italian looming behind Brenda something intensely primeval lurched deep inside her, and her heart flipped over in her chest then dropped like a stone. Wearing an impeccably tailored business suit now, he was enough to stun anyone, and she gaped at him stupidly as he said to Brenda, 'My apologies, *signora*. My business here will take moments only.'

The smooth voice was warm enough to melt frost, the purring quality making Bess's skin curl. And it had an obvious effect on the other woman too, because her, 'I don't allow callers, especially not upstairs,' had lost a hefty dose of vitriol.

'I congratulate you on your good sense.' His white smile seemed to light up the gloomy landing, and Bess couldn't be sure but she thought she saw her landlady simper. She would have found it highly amusing if she hadn't been desperately wondering why she reacted to him the way she did, and trying to work out why he was here, knowing that, whatever the reason, it wouldn't be good. Not for her.

Vaccari said, as if he was sure there could be no objections, 'As I said, my business won't take long. And please don't put yourself to the inconvenience of waiting. I'll see myself out.' And he smoothly inserted his magnificent body into the room, gently but firmly closing the door behind him.

Bess shot to her feet, her heart beating erratically, watching him with wide green eyes as he weighed up the room: the clumsy furniture, the narrow bed.

'A suitable hole for a mouse.' He finished his minute examination and turned tarnished-silver eyes on her, the flickering gleam showing cool amusement. 'Complete with a dragon to make sure the little mouse doesn't stray.'

She made herself ignore that. 'Why are you here?' Her throat felt tight. 'Is Helen with you?' She was probably waiting in his car. Her glamorous sister wouldn't be seen dead in such dull surroundings.

'She's still in Braylington.' His white teeth gleamed. 'She and your mother are deep in port- folios of wedding-dress designs. I don't think either of them will come up for air for at least a fortnight.'

'Oh.' That was all she was able to say. She was drained—suddenly and totally drained. For no good reason. Except that what she had feared had come true.

This man was about to become part of her family. This morning's session with her father made sense now. They had been formally announcing their in- tention to marry, making plans, setting dates.

She wondered acidly if he would be faithful to Helen. Or would he still go around kissing and manhandling all and sundry when the mood took him?

Probably.

Marriage didn't make people change.

'Congratulations,' she forced out, her tongue feeling thick and heavy in her mouth. 'I hope things work out for you both.' She couldn't bring herself to say, I hope you'll be wonderfully happy; she didn't know why, she only knew the words would choke her.

He gave her an odd look then shrugged, as if he thought her stupid. Which, privately, she thought she probably was.

'I wouldn't have agreed to sign the contract if I hadn't been sure,' he said drily. 'Unlike most women, Helen is intelligent, totally trustworthy and single-mindedly dedicated to making a success of the coming change in her life. And so, yes, it will work out. For both of us.'

Suddenly, and for the first time in her life, she felt sorry for Helen. This man would be easy to fall obsessively in love with—provided you didn't look too far beneath the surface, she reminded herself quickly. Did her sister know he regarded their marriage as a contract? That he had only decided to commit himself because he could trust her to devote herself to making him the perfect wife—properly dedicated and single-minded about it?

'Helen apart, you seem to have a very cynical attitude to women,' she told him gruffly, wondering waywardly if he regarded her, along with the rest of the female sex, as stupid, false and vacillating. Wondering why it should hurt.

She saw something hard and sharp in his eyes as he looked at her. 'I have reason to, believe me.' Then he shrugged slightly, as if the subject bored him—or she did—and pushed a hand into his jacket pocket and produced her missing ring.

'Jessica found it in a pile of dirty dishes.' He took her nerveless hand in one of his and dropped the ring into her palm. 'Now, I'd call that a Freudian slip, wouldn't you? Think about it. And think about the things I've said to you. Or not. It's your life.'

He swung gracefully round on the balls of his feet and left, and whether it was because he'd looked as if he was bored silly or because she wanted to call him back and slap him for calling her a mouse she wasn't sure, but she was agitated enough to want to scream the walls down.

Instead, after counting to fifty, forcing herself to calm down a notch or two, she stamped down the stairs and made two decisive phone calls.

# CHAPTER FOUR

'SURE you won't come?' Niccy asked. 'I'll wait while you change.' She was dressed for partying, her beanpole figure looking sensational in scarlet silk leggings topped by a black glittery tunic, and Bess grinned at her, pushing a hand through her rumpled copper hair as she settled more comfortably into the squashy brocade-covered sofa.

'Thanks, but, as I told you, I need a clear head in the morning.' Besides, she had nothing festive to change into.

'If that's really how you feel,' Niccy said thoughtfully. 'But don't get uptight—it's only a new job, remember.'

'I'm not in the least uptight!' Her wide smile backed up her words. 'But we're lunching with some hot-shot financier. Mark's ninety per cent sure he can persuade him to back us. I wouldn't want to wreck his chances by falling asleep!'

The phone buzzed then, and Niccy held out the receiver. 'It's for you. I'll be off if I can't change your mind. Don't wait up.'

Somehow Bess knew it was Tom, and her face flushed a rosy pink as her hunch was confirmed. She felt apprehensive. He'd been so angry when she'd phoned to tell him that she'd decided to take the job and was moving in with Niccy.

'I thought we'd discussed it and decided you'd turn the wretched job down. Tell him you've

45

changed your mind. Let him find some other idiot who's prepared to be made redundant in a couple of months. As for moving from Brenda's—I've never heard anything so stupid. You won't find living with your flashy friend anything like as economical.'

Bess had ignored that. Until they were married she could live where she chose. And she'd reminded him, surprised by the cool steadiness of her voice, '*You* decided I'd turn down the job. I thought it over and decided I'd like the challenge.' Which wasn't exactly true. She hadn't reasoned it out at all, but had acted on impulse, goaded by the way that supercilious Italian had looked at her room and pronounced it a fitting hole for a mouse. 'I've accepted the job and I don't go back on my word. And I don't know why you're so against it.'

'Then you have less common sense than I gave you credit for,' he'd snapped right back. 'And don't bother coming home on my account this weekend. I'll be too busy to see you.'

And that was fine by her, she'd decided, her anger like a slow-burning underground fire. She had her notice to work out, her things to pack ready for the move, and Mark had given her reams of typed information on the properties—small hotels, converted farmhouses, one or two palaces—he intended to sign up if the financial deal went through.

Reading them thoroughly, studying the maps, making notes would keep her busy enough without going home at the weekend to be lectured.

But now maybe he'd had time to simmer down. All the time they'd known each other she'd always gone along with what he suggested, been the type of woman he expected her to be. Having gone directly against his wishes would have come as a shock. She could understand that, and forgive it. But he would have had time to come to terms with that and maybe, just maybe, he was phoning to wish her well in her new career.

'Mother wants to know if you'll be home next weekend,' he said stiffly. 'Aunt Faye's coming to stay. She wants to see you. She took a shine to you when you met, remember? Mother would like you to join us for dinner on Saturday evening.'

'What do *you* want? Do you want me to come?' she asked quietly.

The entire Clayton family treated the irascible old lady as if she were royalty, pussy-footing around her because she was wealthy. She was childless, so they hoped her fortune would go to Tom, and when Bess had made such a good impression they'd all been delighted.

So this weekend they would want to produce her. Newly engaged to Tom, who, despite his best efforts, was not her favourite person, she might be able to keep Aunt Faye's easily ruffled feathers nice and smooth. But he still sounded annoyed with her and she couldn't handle that, not without instigating another fight. And she didn't want to fight with him.

'Of course.' He sounded gruff. 'I'd have thought you'd take that as read. We're engaged, after all.'

Which probably meant he was sorry for the way he'd sounded off when she'd broken the news about the job, and she assured him quickly, her voice softening, 'Then I'll be there.'

'That's my good girl!'

So all was now forgiven, and Bess listened to him tell her how busy he'd been with a sense of relief. She hated being at odds with him; they had never had reason to speak harshly to each other before. And she listened with genuine interest until he mentioned, 'I suppose you know Helen's been spending most of her time here at home? She makes occasional forays into London, but she's been based here since our party. Maybe she's out of work—over the hill as far as top modelling assignments go.'

Had that been said with a tinge of spite? Bess briefly closed her eyes. She must be keeping her wedding plans quiet. She could have explained to Tom, though. He would soon be one of the family, after all—but she couldn't bring herself to mention it.

The thought of Vaccari as her brother-in-law was, against all reason, truly appalling. She didn't want to think about it, much less discuss it. And she'd kept her duty calls home sparse and brief, not giving her mother the opportunity to enthuse about her favourite daughter's wedding plans. So she simply asked, 'Is that a problem?' and went on to talk of other things, and only when she finally put the phone down could she begin to ease away the unwelcome, nagging tension and put her mind to deciding what to wear for that all-important business lunch tomorrow.

As the taxi stopped at traffic lights Bess plucked a mirror from her bag and checked her appearance. Her glossy hair was neatly subdued, her make-up discreet, the collar of her oyster silk blouse tidily tucked away beneath the lapels of her taupe wool suit.

While she was putting the mirror away the taxi surged forward, and her eyes fell on the slim leather briefcase containing the Jenson business proposals. No need to feel nervous, she told herself. Although she would have been happier to arrive at the restaurant with Mark. But he'd been tied up in a meeting with his bank manager for most of the morning and was relying on her to be at the restaurant on time, to hold the fort if the unpredictable happened and he was delayed.

Which she was perfectly happy to do—if only she'd remembered to ask the financier's name! But she could fudge her way round that one, she told herself calmly as she paid off the taxi when it drew up outside one of the city's most sumptuous restaurants.

She'd done her homework and had every reason to have confidence in her ability to make a useful contribution to the coming meeting, and wasn't too perturbed when she was told that, no, Mr Jenson had not yet arrived, but their guest was already seated.

A discreet consultation with her wristwatch told her she was exactly three minutes late. She'd been sure that she'd left herself loads of time, but the traffic had been horrendous. Formulating an apology, she adjured herself to smile as she followed the *maître d'* on through, and was swamped by a truly awful sense of cruel inevitability when Luke Vaccari rose to greet her.

'I'm—I'm sorry I'm late,' she floundered childishly, sinking down abruptly as a waiter held out her chair. Her stomach clenched convulsively. Of all the backers available, why had Mark had to approach Vaccari?

'A few moments only,' he soothed urbanely, his silver eyes glimmering at her beneath the thick black tangle of his lashes. 'When Jenson contacted me to say he might be held up, he assured me that his PA, Bess Ryland, would look after me.'

He leaned back in his chair, his dark head tipped slightly to one side, his smile wickedly amused as he murmured, 'There could be two Bess Rylands involved in the travel business, but I decided the coincidence would be too great. So that assurance of his spiced the small waiting time with delightful anticipation. So here we are, Bess.' His smile was positively wicked now. 'I'm ready and willing—look after me nicely.'

She loathed the undercurrent of innuendo and strove to ignore it. She stared straight back at him, making her face controlled and still. If she had her way, she'd look after him with a double-barrelled shotgun! she thought caustically. But this meeting was too important to Mark to do or say anything that might jeopardise his chances of securing the financial backing he needed if his new business was to grow.

'Of course,' she replied tonelessly, determinedly taking his words at face value. 'We won't order until Mark arrives, but I'm sure you'd like a drink.'

'I already have one.' A slant of silver eyes indicated the untouched glass of wine, and even though his face was perfectly straight Bess was painfully aware that he was laughing at her.

'I—I hadn't noticed.' She had the feeling she was being tested. And had failed. In her agitation she'd noticed nothing but his unwelcome presence. How easily he could make her feel foolish!

She unknotted her fingers and reached for the briefcase. 'I have our proposal here. You might like to glance at it while we wait.' With his attention fixed on facts and figures, away from her, she would be able to breathe more easily.

But he replied disconcertingly, 'I've already studied it in detail.' His wide shoulders lifted in an elegantly casual, dismissive shrug. "To agree to a meeting without having done so would be a waste of my time. I don't waste time, Bess.'

She knew that. To her cost, she knew that. They had barely met before he had deliberately set out to unsettle her. Recalling the acid-sweet taunts, the way he'd touched her, kissed her, made her head swim, her muscles clench with tension.

And all the time he'd been planning to marry her sister! And she hadn't had a second's real peace of mind since.

She made an effort to push it all out of her head, but it was impossible, and when he said softly, 'Relax, Bess,' she raised haunted green eyes to his, unconsciously pleading, begging him to let her be.

But if he'd read the desperate message he clearly had no intention of accommodating her. There was an amused curl to his cruel, sensual mouth as he watched her intently, musing, 'Helen told me you were a very humble secretary in a branch of a travel agency chain. Yet you turn up as PA to a young man who's going places fast. Has she always denigrated your achievements?'

'Of course not,' Bess denied untruthfully. But she had grown used to being constantly put down, being compared unfavourably with her gorgeous, vivacious sister. It didn't bother her really, hadn't done since she'd begun to understand that nobody consciously wanted to hurt her.

Besides, Helen had obviously given the information before she'd accepted the job with Mark. And Helen was her sister. She wasn't going to say a word against her to the man she was soon to marry; she wasn't that small-minded.

'Today's my first day with Mark,' she admitted tensely, then was furious with herself for giving him the opportunity to gloat as he purred with what sounded like monumental self-congratulation,

'Then you did take my advice. You decided to try your wings. Good for you, Bess.'

His conceit took her breath away, disabling her. She wished she could think of something swift and cutting to put him in his place.

And it wasn't true. The way he'd called her room at Brenda's a mousehole might, to some degree, have been responsible for catapulting her into the decision to share with Niccy. She would, reluctantly, admit to that. But no way had her decision to work for Mark had anything to do with him! Faced so unexpectedly with him again, she had to make herself believe that.

She almost whimpered with relief when Mark finally joined them. She was safe now—safe from whatever it was that Vaccari did to her.

A shudder coursed down her backbone. She didn't like herself when the Italian was around and the feeling was difficult to cope with. But she had to cope; right now she had to. For Mark's sake.

And to begin with it was easier than she had dared hope. Vaccari's questions and comments were incisive, indicating clearly that, however lightweight his attitudes might be when it came to his emotional life, he was undeviatingly single-minded in his business affairs. And Mark put his case convincingly, his narrow, clever face enthusiastic, enabling Bess to forget her animosity and make a few telling points of her own, so that she was almost sorry when Vaccari was called away to the phone.

He rose from the table with a graceful apology and Mark leaned towards her, his eyes bright with confidence. 'That just about wraps it up, I think. We haven't left anything out, have we?'

'I can't think of anything.' Bess broke into a grin because she too felt buoyantly confident. Given that Vaccari was the backer Mark had approached, the whole meeting had been easier than she could have hoped. Strangely exhilarating too. The Italian had done his homework, she had to give him that, and she knew they'd put their case convincingly. 'Will he give us a decision now, or will we have to wait and bite our nails down to our knuckles?'

'Now, I hope. I'll push for it, anyway.' He glanced quickly over his shoulder then turned back to Bess. 'Tell me if I'm wrong, but I got the impression at one point that you and Vaccari know each other from somewhere.'

Sighing, Bess felt her elation wither away. She knew the incident he was talking about. A lull in a discussion of cash-flow requirements while their fish-course plates had been whisked away had

brought those tarnished-silver eyes homing in on
the slender fingers of her left hand.

'You haven't managed to lose the ring perma-
nently, then. If I were writing a progress report I'd
say "Must try harder".'

As if she'd deliberately left her ring in the dirty
dishes! And she had no intention of breaking up
with Tom, as he had suggested—he had to know
that! He couldn't help making snide remarks, nasty
comments, and she'd been sorely tempted to tell
him to mind his own damn business, but had been
saved from that folly by the smooth arrival of the
next course. Then Mark had taken up the earlier
discussion, and to her sagging relief the Italian had
given his unwavering attention over to business
again.

'He's going to marry my sister,' she said stiltedly
now. 'I hardly know him at all.'

'Luke Vaccari marry again?' Mark's eyes popped
wide open. 'Bang goes his reputation!'

'Reputation?' Bess parroted, as if the word had
a nasty taste, and Mark lifted one shoulder.

He told her, 'You know what it's like with these
wealthy workaholics. What play time they get is
quality time. Plenty of lovely ladies to pick and
choose from, nothing but the very best, but no
commitment—definitely no commitment. In his
case, given his background, I'd say he couldn't trust
a woman under fifty as far as he could throw her.'
Then, catching the disgust in her huge emerald eyes,
he coloured uncomfortably. 'Forget I spoke. Your
sister must be a wonderful woman. And don't forget
it's said that reformed rakes make the most faithful husbands—

'Oh, no problems, I hope?' Mark turned with obvious relief as the 'rake', reformed or not, returned to the table. 'More coffee?'

Luke shook his head to both, leaning back in his chair and looking every inch the man in charge as his eyes idled from Bess to Mark and back to Bess again.

Her skin tautened with explicable tension and something hot and dark jerked savagely in the pit of her stomach as those veiled silver eyes minutely studied her face, feature by feature. And then, as if pulling himself from some private reverie, he drawled softly, 'I'm impressed by your package, Jenson. Call by my Lombard Street office tomorrow and my finance and legal department will draw up a contract.

'But there is one thing.' His voice was low, a husky purr, his eyes on Bess again. She shivered. She felt—unreasonably, she hoped—as if she was waiting for a catastrophe to happen. He looked almost sinister, but she couldn't look away as his eyes bored more deeply into hers. 'A favour,' he said.

'Of course—anything!'

Bess just knew her boss was having difficulty containing his elation. If they hadn't been in a public place he'd have leapt to his feet and punched the air.

She desperately wanted to warn him to be careful, but knew she couldn't, knew he wouldn't listen if she did. But he didn't know Vaccari as she did. The 'favour' he was about to ask could be dynamite, and Mark, tumbling over himself to agree to anything, couldn't see that.

'From your proposal I see Ms Ryland's first brief is to travel to Tuscany on Wednesday of this week to set up deals and itineraries at two locations you personally vetted while on a scouting trip last autumn.'

'That's right.' Mark leaned forward eagerly. 'A converted convent on the outskirts of Florence and a—'

'I would like you to consider a third,' Vaccari cut in smoothly. 'I have a cousin—a widow, sadly. Her husband left her a small castle and many debts. I offered to discharge them.' He shrugged, his distinctive features bland. 'But Emilia is independent.

'However, when she announced her intention of putting her inheritance to good use, she agreed to allow me to finance her. The castle is to be made into a small, exclusive hotel—permission has been granted, architects engaged. If, after her Tuscan business is finished, Ms Ryland would meet me there—shall we say Saturday?—and give me an opinion on whether, on completion, Emilia's hotel would meet Jenson's exacting standards we would be eternally grateful.'

His heavy-lidded eyes mocked her sudden hectic colour. It was as if he knew the reason for the instinctive clench of fear that took her breath away. The fear was real enough, but the reason for it lay worryingly beyond her grasp. So why should his eyes tell her that he understood it perfectly?

It made her feel diminished, lacking in a sense of self, all her control gone, given over to him.

And, precisely as she had known he would, Mark agreed.

'Done! If it works out, we all benefit. The more tempting venues I can offer the better. It depends, of course, but if your cousin could get the place up and running in time we could feature it in our brochures next year.'

He was talking as if the proposed hotel would have everything going for it—style, location, excellence of service, Bess thought irritably. But then, of course, he would bend over backwards to please his new backer. And never mind if the last thing she wanted was to meet up with him on Saturday.

Saturday!

Bess squirmed in her seat. Tom was counting on her being home this weekend. Never mind Aunt Faye's fortune: the old lady could leave everything to the exchequer to help reduce the national debt for all she cared. But Tom had said he wanted her there, putting them back on their old, comfortable, footing, the disagreement over her job forgotten. She wasn't prepared to disappoint him. So she said firmly, 'I'm sorry. I've made arrangements for this weekend. They'd be difficult to cancel.'

'But not impossible?'

She heard the confidence in his voice and hated him for it, despised his tactics, too, when Mark jumped on her.

'Nothing's impossible.' His eyes snapped a message that only a fool would have ignored—all to do with the short shelf-life of new assistants who refused to cancel a social arrangement to accommodate the whims of the man who held the purse-strings. 'Fax me the details of the location, the time you wish to meet, and Bess will be at your disposal.'

Stuck between a rock and a hard place, Bess could only capitulate. She had no choice—not if she wanted to avoid the dole queue and the inevitable 'I told you so's from Tom.

'Ms Ryland?' Tiny flames of triumph leapt in the depths of the Italian's eyes. The choice he appeared to be offering was no choice at all. And he knew it.

'As Mark says, I am at your disposal,' she conceded stiffly, her face set. He had got his own way, as he had known he would, but she didn't have to smile about it.

# CHAPTER FIVE

HIGH in the hills to the north-east of Florence, Bess slowed down and glanced at the sheet of directions on the passenger seat of her hired car.

Satisfied that she really was meant to take the unmade track snaking away on her left, she pulled the car into the side of the narrow road and gave herself a few moments to get herself mentally in tune for the coming meeting with Luke Vaccari and his cousin.

The two and a half days she'd spent giving the two hotels Mark intended to sign up a detailed inspection—from the quality of the cuisine down to the reliability of the plumbing—had been hectic. And back in her room in the evenings she'd worked on her written reports until she could have sworn her eyes were about to drop out.

And even then she hadn't been able to sleep because of the guilt she'd felt over letting Tom down. His reaction to the news that she wouldn't be able to fit in a visit and see Aunt Faye was something she didn't want to dwell on. It hadn't been flattering and she'd had the strongest suspicion that he'd been more interested in keeping the rich old lady sweet than seeing his brand-new fiancée.

And, as if that wasn't enough, there'd been this squirmy feeling inside her every time she'd thought about seeing Vaccari again. And, if she was totally honest with herself, she had to admit that the sensation had been more akin to excitement than apprehension.

She didn't know what was wrong with her and groaned softly, closing her eyes, her teeth worrying at the corner of her mouth.

She hated the way he made her feel. She didn't want it. He did something to her that she couldn't control. It was, she told herself grittily as she put the car into gear, an experience she could have lived without.

She took what comfort she could from the fact that they wouldn't be alone together. His cousin would be around and that, hopefully, would stem his wicked, unsettling taunts and quite definitely put paid to his hands-on approach, because Emilia would surely know about his wedding plans and he wouldn't want news of his sneaky misdemeanours getting back to his wife-to-be, who was rapturously trying to choose her wedding gown!

If this was the only access to the proposed hotel then the surface would have to be greatly improved, she noted, pushing her brain into business mode, then jumped on the brakes because Luke Vaccari strolled round the first bend, his hands stuffed in the pockets of the casual white chinos he wore.

Her skin went damp. It had been only a few days since she had seen him last yet the mere sight of him was a cataclysmic shock to her system. It made her mouth go dry, her heart beat like a steam-hammer. She hated him for his ability to do this to her, despised herself for reacting to his raw sexuality like a silly adolescent.

It was only a passing aberration, she told herself raggedly as he walked round and slid his long, indolent body into the passenger seat. It had to be. Her mind had been in a turmoil, one way or another, ever since they'd met, and now her body had joined in the fun—wanting to touch and be touched, wanting to be held, closely held, wanting a repetition of the kiss that had rocked her to the foundations of her being, wanting all the forbidden, wicked things...

'I decided to meet you,' he explained lightly, angling himself in his seat to face her. 'After a few hundred yards you could have decided you'd taken the wrong turn-off and turned back. And got lost. I wouldn't want to lose you—such a little thing in such a large landscape.'

He was doing it again, she agonised, her heart contracting painfully. Making her feel important, of value, making her believe—

She forced the thought roughly away. It made her shake. He wasn't smiling and the dark glasses he wore hid his eyes, and his black shirt made his skin tones more olive. His voice was soft as he instructed, 'Drive on, Bess.'

So, fumblingly, she did, stingingly aware of his dark-veiled gaze. And that heightened her awareness of everything else: the folds of the hills, the blues, the greens, the distant purples; the shining loop of a river far below; the heat of the sun, the heat of her body, the molten heat inside her, the sudden distaste for the plain cotton skirt and blouse she'd chosen to travel in.

Flames performed a searing dance in the pit of her stomach and she took a bend in the track far too fast, slowed down a little, her heart thumping wildly, and tried to pull herself together, to pretend that Vaccari was a million miles away.

And she thought about Tom—or tried to. But he eluded her; she couldn't bring his face to mind, so she wondered if he'd still be angry when she was next able to visit home and found it didn't worry her as much as it should have done.

'How much further?' she asked, her voice thick. The sooner this visit was over the better she'd feel.

And she heard him say, 'We are already there.' The soft hint of amusement in his voice made her fingers curl more tightly round the wheel as he added, 'Not before time. The—flamboyance?—of your driving makes me wonder if my life-insurance policy is up to date.'

To tell him that normally she was a safe, responsible driver, that his presence alone made her drive like a novice trying to emulate Damon Hill on the racetrack, would give far too much away. If he knew how he could affect her he would take advantage, wouldn't he? And besides, she was momentarily robbed of the power of speech as the car skidded round a final bend, scattering stones.

The *castello* wasn't at all how she'd imagined it. It was no sprawling, ruinous pile but a place of golden beauty, perched on a plateau where a garden had been made, making the ancient building look as if it was floating on a cloud of greenery. It had four square towers, a great central door, and a naïvety and charm that made her catch her breath.

'It's lovely.' Enchanted, she forgot for a moment why she was here and who she was with. 'Out of this world.'

'Then Jenson's clients should be suitably impressed,' he remarked, his eyes on her enraptured face—and quickly reminded her of what she was doing here.

She straightened her smile out quickly and drove on, more carefully now, getting herself back under control as she followed the track that wound round, gently climbing the plateau until it reached a huge sweep of stony forecourt in front of the main door. There she cut the engine, stating, 'The access road would have to be paved. Although Jenson's put a car and a driver at our clients' disposal for the duration of their stay, some of them do like to drive themselves some of the time.'

She undid her seat belt and slid out of the car, feeling practically together again, waiting while he unfolded himself from the passenger seat and joined her before adding, even more coolly, 'The track doesn't meet with our standards.'

The words slipped out decisively, letting him know—politely, of course—that there were high standards to be met, even if he did hold the purse-strings.

And she was doing fine, showing him she was a professional. She felt justifiably proud of herself and fully intended to keep it up for the few hours she would need to be here. But then his hooded eyes made an inventory of her appearance, no doubt taking in her travel-wrinkled, boring clothes, her sensible flat shoes, the sweat-dampened hair that was coming adrift from its moorings.

His mouth curling unforgivably, he murmured, 'So the mouse has grown sharp fangs. Well done, *carissima*, well done!'

Colour flooded her face, which made her feel more unkempt and gauche than ever, and the impulse to retaliate, to slap his handsome, unrepentant face, was almost too strong to be ignored. But she recalled how he'd responded to her previous bout of uncharacteristic violence and brought herself back in line, turning from him to retrieve her handbag from the rear seat, stiffening slightly when he asked, 'Your luggage? Open the boot and I'll carry it in.'

She dragged in a sharp breath then told him levelly, 'That won't be necessary,' guiltily reminded that the directions that had been faxed through had also mentioned overnight accommodation. Emilia would have been put to the trouble of getting a room ready for her for nothing. She would apologise to her. 'All I need to do at this stage is see the plans and discuss the potential. The rest—ease of access to places of interest and so on—can be done from my office.'

With any luck, she thought, hitching the strap of her bag over her shoulder, she could be on her way back to Florence well before nightfall—keeping everything nice and polite here, making a few suggestions, a few vague promises for Mark's sake, then beating a dignified retreat.

'Actually—' she dug her notebook from her bag '—I planned on getting to Pisa airport this evening.' So that she could be back in Braylington by tomorrow lunchtime and mollify Tom, although, thinking about it, that didn't seem nearly as important as removing herself from Vaccari's presence.

But she wasn't going to think of the implications of that. She didn't dare. And his silent, probing scrutiny wasn't helping any so she snapped, 'Shall we make a start?' and quivered inside as she watched him smile, tipping his head consideringly on one side.

'Why the hurry, *cara*? We have plenty of time. Why rush back to England where it is sure to be raining? My homeland is beautiful—why don't you relax, enjoy? Throw away your business hat; it's very new, after all. Surely it pinches—just a little?'

His smile was too tempting; it made her ache. Yet she wanted to tear those dark glasses away and read his expression. It would be mocking. He would be laughing at her for trying to stamp her professionalism on this meeting, still seeing her as that mousy creature who always did as she was told.

He was getting more Italian by the moment. More dangerous. Or was the danger within herself, stemming from the way her senses responded to him like a tightly furled blossom unfolding towards the sun?

'My time isn't my own, remember?' she got out past the sudden tightness in her throat. 'The business is expanding and Mark and I both have venues to vet all over Europe; we can't afford to spend too much time on a place that isn't up and running yet. You'll understand that.'

Her green eyes all but begged him to understand, to allow her the small victory of retreat. She knew she wasn't much good at hiding her real feelings and was suddenly truly desperate enough not to care.

Her pride was no longer important—let him understand the way she was beginning to feel about him if that was what it took. No, her pride wasn't important but her self-respect was. How could she live with herself if she didn't limit the time she spent with him to the utmost minimum? If she allowed him time to make her feel things she shouldn't feel, want things she shouldn't want? And he could do that so easily, just by being there.

He dipped his head just slightly, his smile enigmatic, then strode across the courtyard, leaving her to follow. She didn't know if he intended to cooperate—to hurry things up and let her go—or not. Whether he thought it safer, wiser, because he knew she was falling in love—

With a brutal spurt of mental energy she knocked the thought down. What he did to her was basic chemistry. A silly little innocent's untutored reaction to the force of raw, primitive, shameless sex appeal. She was in love with Tom, wasn't she? What she felt for Vaccari was nothing more elevated than lust, the temptation of the forbidden.

She closed her eyes briefly, a knot in her throat, rooted to the spot as sudden lethargy rolled over her in waves. The temptation to do what he had suggested—relax and enjoy—was immense. The warmth of the sun stroked her body, the golden heat tempered by the soft, herb-scented breeze. Her hazy eyes fastened on him as he walked away, and clung, devouring the strong, elegant lines of him, and she knew it would be all too easy to stay, go with the drift of the moment, take what might happen . . .

But she was stronger than that. She walked after him, trying to push everything out of her mind except the need to put one foot in front of the other, and caught up with him as he opened a narrow door set into the much larger, heavy oak main entrance.

Thick, honey-coloured stone walls created a dim tunnel, emerging into a blaze of light that was a central courtyard, with stone towers at each corner and the arches of a cool loggia stretching in between.

It was like stepping into a fantasy world... dangerous—as dangerous as the man at her side, because what he could make her feel was a fantasy too. She gave a sigh that was next-of-kin to a sob of relief as a rotund lady in black emerged from between one of the arches—she was no longer alone with him in this magical place, pulled to him by the dark enchantment that she was determined to will out of existence if she could.

But the relief was short-lived. He spoke to the woman in rapid Italian and she responded with what looked suspiciously like a bobbing curtsey then trotted away, so she couldn't be, as Bess had initially thought, his cousin, Emilia.

'Chiara will bring us something cool to drink,' he told her. 'Come.' The casual sweep of his hand indicated the direction and she went unwillingly, achingly conscious of him at her side as they passed through the shade of the loggia and into a great vaulted hall where the marble slabs were cool and echoing beneath her feet.

There was a staircase that seemed to soar to the ceiling, two massive stone fireplaces, and stone doorways which eventually led to yet another sunny loggia, this one open to the view of the countryside and the garden upon which the castle had seemed to float when she'd seen it from the road.

He led the way over the marble paving slabs to a group of upholstered cane chairs and a long, low table which already bore a tall jug of iced lemonade and a bowl of fruit.

'Your employer will allow you to rest for ten minutes, take a little refreshment?' A lean hand gestured sweepingly to one of the chairs and Bess knew he was mocking her, taking her earlier words and stuffing them, oh, so elegantly, down her throat.

There was nothing she could do to counter that. She would make herself look ridiculous if she refused. Besides, she was thirsty. Taking care to sound calm and collected, she sank into the chair and remarked, 'This is beautiful. Like a lovely outdoor room.' There were statues along the terrace and a rampant mass of wistaria, cascades of soft pink roses tumbling over the edge, foaming into the garden below.

But her surroundings faded into nothing as she raised her eyes to find him watching her. He was so beautiful. She wanted to reach out and touch him, trace the sensual line of his mouth with her fingers, close those tarnished-silver eyes with hot kisses . . .

Her fingers curled into her palms and her breath snagged in her throat because what she was feeling was insanity. He belonged to Helen and she belonged to Tom . . .

But she didn't want Tom . . . .

'I'm glad you've found something of which you can approve,' he said drily, and she forced her mind back from the brink, fixing her eyes on the view as he took the chair opposite hers, stretching out his long legs. She tried to batten down panic as he added, 'But don't reach for your clipboard yet. There is ample time.'

Time to compound her own foolishness, she thought grimly. Time was what she didn't want. With every second she spent in his company the tug of his physical magnetism grew stronger, drawing her into the abyss.

She had to get away, and soon. The fluttery panic was intensifying. She forced some lemonade down, the ice clinking against the side of the glass—an audible testament to her shaky hands—and told him, 'I'd like to meet your cousin now and make a start on what I'm here to do.'

And she felt as if she'd been punched in her stomach when he gave her that devastating, lazy smile and said, 'Didn't I explain? Emilia is in Switzerland for her health. The death of her husband, her stubborn determination to be independent and tussles with the planning authorities left her in a state of collapse. So she is away, resting, leaving me to do the honours.' As he got languidly to his feet Bess wrapped her arms tightly around her body, holding herself together.

The silver innocence of those eyes didn't fool her. Of course he hadn't told her they'd be here alone.

She'd cope, though. She would have to. The only person she had to fear was herself. There was no real danger from him. So he'd kissed her, been more familiar than he had any right to be. And he couldn't help flirting; it was in his Italian genes. But he didn't mean anything by it. How could he be remotely interested in her when he would soon be marrying her gorgeous sister?

She looked at him from deeply troubled eyes as he said, '*Scusi*. There's something I have to attend to before we make a start.'

He walked away and she closed her eyes to stop them devouring the lithe and economical movements of his body, then snapped them open and stood up, wanting to get herself sorted out for his return.

After trying unsuccessfully to smooth the creases from her skirt, she resignedly gave up and smoothed down her hair instead, twisting the wayward coppery curls and securing them firmly with the pins, and took some pride in the way she was able to take her notepad in her hand and start to walk towards him as soon as he reappeared at the end of the terrace.

'Perhaps you would show me the plans?' she suggested levelly, refusing to allow herself the luxury of looking at him directly, pinning her gaze on one of the statues instead. 'That's all I need to do at this stage. There can be a proper inspection when it's fully functioning as a hotel.'

Neat, she told herself. Very neat. A sensible-sounding way of making her time here as short as possible.

And she didn't suspect a thing when he told her, 'I have Mark on the phone for you. In the small *salone*. Come, I'll show you the way.'

It was an airy room with a painted, carved-wood ceiling, and she took up the receiver, sure that her boss was merely checking that she'd arrived safely, had everything in hand, possibly having instructions for what he wanted her to do on Monday, back at the office—especially if he intended to be away.

But two seconds into the conversation was enough to have the colour draining from her face, her knuckles showing white through her skin as her grip tightened on the instrument.

'Listen—I gather you've got the idea you can only afford to spend a couple of hours on the Vaccari job. Well, you can forget that, Bess.' He sounded far from pleased and she caught a definite threat in his voice as he added, 'Apart from the distinct possibility of the property becoming a valuable asset on our lists, the man's goodwill is vitally important to us at this stage. He's to be given total co-operation. Get that? If he wants you to stay a week, going over everything with a magnifying glass, then you'll do it. And that's an order.'

# CHAPTER SIX

BESS was angry. Scorchingly angry. Did he get a kick out of making her dance to his tune? Could he guess what was happening to her? Did he think it was funny?

She was also angry with herself for getting into a situation where it actually mattered!

She spun on the heels of her sensible flat shoes, but there was nothing sensible at all about the way she snapped at him, 'Been telling tales, have you? What wouldn't you stoop to to get your own way? You could have cost me my job, do you realise that?'

As soon as the words erupted she knew they were way over the top, and the loose shrug he gave her, the eloquent way he spread his hands, was a silent, humiliating confirmation.

'You do me an injustice, *cara*.' The words slid out like warm dark honey, sending rough shivers down her back, and his eyes were laughing. 'I wanted to put your mind at rest, that was all. You appeared to believe you're expected to rush around like a tornado, while I knew Mark would want you to take your time, make a thorough inspection.'

He shot her his sudden, wickedly irresistible smile. 'Regard the time you spend here as a working holiday. And, while you're at it, try to relax. You're doing just fine. When you turned out to be Jenson's PA I wanted to give you a medal. And that initial meeting confirmed what I'd suspected—you're bright as a button and not afraid of concentrated work. Mark didn't hire you to make the tea, so he's not going to fire you for one error of judgement.'

And who was responsible for that error of judgement? she fumed inwardly. He was!

He had picked her out from the crowd, tormented her, teased her, flattered and flirted, scrambled her brain and made her feel things she didn't want to feel, had no right to feel.

So it was all his fault!

And his patronising 'I wanted to give you a medal' had hit a raw nerve and she ground out, without thinking, 'No need to pat yourself on the back. I didn't take the job with Mark because of anything you said, so don't think it! And if you're thinking of repeating your *advice*—' she invested the word with withering scorn '—that I break with Tom you can save your breath because it's none of your business, is it?'

And, too late, she wished she'd held her tongue because he grinned at her, his arms folded over his impressive chest, murmuring throatily, 'Take note— I didn't mention your dull fiancé. You did. It is something we're going to have to work on. Together. And now we have the time, don't we?' His devilish smile widened. 'All the time we need. But one step at a time. I rush nothing. Nothing— you understand?'

All the while he'd been speaking his eyes had made a languid inspection of her body, mentally stripping away her crumpled, unappealing clothes, so she'd have had to be brain-dead not to understand, wouldn't she?

He intended to continue the flirting game. Because it amused him? Amused him to see his mousy soon-to-be-sister-in-law go all dewy-eyed and weak at the knees? Or was he intending to put another notch on his bedpost while he was still legally, if not morally, free to do so?

The very thought of that started a conflagration deep inside her. She hated him for the power he had and wondered wildly if, in the years to come, he would smile at her at some family gathering, his eyes inviting her to remember...

'*Cara*—what's wrong?'

She came out of the storm of her raging thoughts to drown in the silver of his eyes. Compassionate eyes. And regretful? Whatever, she couldn't stand it. He reached out a hand to touch her face and she flung her head back savagely, not daring to accept the contact, and managed, 'I'm annoyed over the way you pushed me into spending more time here than I can afford. But don't worry, I can live with that.'

'I'm glad to hear it,' he said drily, in the same breath adding, 'The arrangements you'd made for this weekend and had to cancel—did they include Tom?'

'As it happens, yes.'

'And that troubles you? Makes you unable to relax?'

'No. It doesn't trouble me.' And that, she recognised, was the truth.

It had bothered her to begin with, given her sleepless nights. Having to explain she'd be away when Tom had expressly asked her to be home this weekend had troubled her deeply. But it had suddenly occurred to her that Tom would never have cancelled a meeting with a client—no matter how exasperating the client or inconvenient the timing—on her account. Business was business, as he'd always maintained. So at least she no longer felt guilty about that.

What she did feel guilty about was the way this man could make her feel.

Pushing that go-nowhere thought aside, she fished her car keys from her handbag and tossed them to him, her mouth tight with annoyance as she said, 'So I'm staying. It's no big deal. Bring the suitcase from the boot and then you can show me my room. I'd like to freshen up since there's apparently no hurry to get down to work.'

For the first time in their odd relationship she actually had the upper hand, she thought spikily as she watched him walk away, tossing the keys idly from one hand to the other.

If only she could keep it up. To keep herself safe from the shocking power he wielded over her senses, to keep her integrity intact, she had to put him in his place and very firmly keep him there.

But thinking about it, watching him, there was something suspicious about that lazy, slightly swaggering walk. Something that clanged a few warning bells, imprinted a puzzled frown between her brows.

And all was made clear when, a few minutes later, a wrinkle-faced little man trotted towards her with her suitcase in one hand and her briefcase in the other, and it was Chiara who emerged to show her to her room, introducing Alfredo as her husband, imparting in her fractured English, 'Signor Vaccari

is saying you to—to—must rest. To wait on him
for *la cena—più tardi*—capire?'

She tipped her head on one side, wrinkling her
nose at Bess's baffled incomprehension, before a
big beaming smile lit up her friendly face. 'Food.
*L'ora—nove.*' She held up nine fingers, nodding,
willing Bess to understand.

She did, and nodded bleakly. So much for getting
the upper hand. She was to hang around until he
condescended to see her again—for the evening
meal at nine o'clock!

He had effectually taught her not to toss orders
at him and expect him to knuckle under.

He was in control, and knowing that did nothing
to settle her racing pulses, but the room she had
been given was beautiful, and she made herself
concentrate on that to take her mind off him and
his wicked manipulations.

The boards beneath her feet had been polished
to a high gloss and sunlight shimmered on white
walls, while the wooden ceiling was richly painted
with strange birds and flowers, and the headboard
of the enormous bed was ornately gilded and decorated with cherubs, roses and spectacularly well-
endowed naked ladies.

And if it hadn't been so obviously a priceless an-
tique she would probably have blushed to the roots
of her hair.

The silent, mental battle she'd been waging
against the forbidden attraction, the desperately
dangerous slide into becoming deeply infatuated
with Luke Vaccari, had depleted her energy until it
was virtually non-existent and the bed looked so

inviting, so wickedly, decadently sumptuous, and she had hours to kill...

Knowing she should be firm with herself and use the time to finish writing up her notes on the Florence trip wasn't enough to stop her stretching out on the white counterpane, just for a moment or two, closing her eyes to rest them for a few seconds, and opening them drowsily to find the room shrouded in blue dusk, the only illumination the soft glow of a bedside lamp, the diffused light lovingly delineating the features that stopped her heart, the tall, powerful body that made primitive need kick into raw life deep inside her.

Luke. She didn't know whether she breathed his name out loud; she only knew that the battle had been fought and lost.

She was in love with the man who was about to marry her sister.

She had committed the ultimate folly. The feeling swamped her. The pain was sharp, physical, inescapable, and she turned her head into the pillow to stifle the building sob of anguished self-disgust, but he leaned forward, long fingers capturing her chin, his touch sending charges of electrical current through her bones, his voice lapping her with warmth, with a desperate longing to reach out for him as he told her, 'Chiara is busy with dinner. I came to show you the way down. You must have been exhausted, *cara*, to sleep so soundly.'

Idly almost, he stroked the smooth curve of her cheek with the backs of his fingers and a long, trembling shudder built up deep inside her body. She gritted her teeth, barely able to contain the spiralling ache of yearning.

And when the tips of his fingers touched the corner of her mouth she twisted her head away savagely again and wrenched herself up against the pillows, and he misread the cause of her panic—obviously he did—because he straightened up, reassuring her, 'The meal will keep for ten minutes or so. Don't worry about it. Have your shower while I sort out something fresh for you to slip into—it will save time.'

Uncomfortably aware of her crumpled state, she slid off the bed. Thankfully, he'd put the wrong interpretation on her flurry of panic. Saving time wasn't her priority. And although he was acting like her big brother now she trusted neither him nor herself and she definitely didn't want him going through her things. She couldn't cope with that kind of intimacy.

'There's no need for that,' she said stiffly, unaware of the naked fright in her wide green eyes, but he was aware and he mentally shook his head, doing his best to make her feel less threatened as he told her wryly, 'I don't have a fetish about women's underwear. Now scoot—you're wasting time.'

She went, simply because she couldn't stay. Being in the same room, breathing the same air, constricted her blood vessels, made her heart pound.

How could she have let her emotions get so out of hand? she agonised as she closed the bathroom door behind her and leant defeatedly against it. There was no lock, she noted, her brows bunching together as panic fluttered crazily through her again, right down to her toes, making them curl against the cool marble floor.

How could the human heart behave so destructively? How could it act in such a way? Falling in love with her sister's future husband was the most senseless thing she had ever done. It made her feel deeply, shamefully guilty and utterly stupid!

And it also meant that she couldn't marry Tom.

Well, how could she? Even if a miracle happened and she fell out of love with Luke immediately she would always remember. Remember and compare.

Remember things she would rather forget, would have been better off never knowing. Remember the way she trembled inside when he looked at her and smiled, the way she had to do physical battle with herself to stop her arms reaching out for him. Remember the awful aching need to be close to him always... always...

She had never, ever felt like that about Tom. Never felt that the merest sight of him made life more glowing, more intense, richer, more worth living.

Beginning to shake all over, she did her best to batten down the clamouring emotions that were in danger of pulling her to pieces and shucked off her clothes with unsteady hands while casting an anxious glance at the door.

Her shower would have to be one of the shortest on record. She didn't think he'd actually invade her privacy to the extent of walking in here, and the smoked-glass shower stall would afford some protection, but intimacy of any kind—even the casual, natural-seeming kind that he'd brought with him when he'd come to wake her—would be too much for her poor demented heart to bear.

So she was out within three minutes, wrapped in a bathsheet, dragging the plastic shower cap from her head when he walked through as if he had every right, draping the clothes he'd had the gall to pick out on a padded stool, not looking at her, not once, striding back out again with an easy, 'Five minutes. OK?'

It would have to be. Although dinner with him was something she didn't know how she'd get through. And her face felt hot, every bone in her body quaking as she reached out a hand for the tumble of black fabric, the lacy briefs and sheer, sheer tights.

Her eyes closed on a groan of bleak despair. What on earth had possessed her? What had made her rush out to buy on a wild impulse after she'd learned she'd be meeting up with Luke this weekend? What had made her splurge out on a deep flame-coloured top and trousers which she was sure she would never have the courage to wear, and this—the sexy black chiffon shift with the silver-beaded embroidery round the hem and the indecently scooped neckline?

And trust him to pick it out in preference to the sensible things she'd brought along—the practical cotton skirts and tops, the neat shirtwaister in go-anywhere beige.

Padding back into the bedroom wrapped in a towel to retrieve the shirtwaister wasn't an option. He would accuse her of wasting time again, argue, ask her if she was afraid to wear the black dress, and all the time she would be searingly conscious of him, of her nakedness, of the shameful, guilty desire to have him remove the towel, touch her, stroke the contours of her body with his eyes, pull her into his arms...

She blanked out the insanity of her thoughts ruthlessly and dressed quickly, refusing to look at herself in one of the many mirrors as she brushed her hair.

It would have to stay loose around her shoulders. Her fingers had turned to thumbs and there was no way she could manage to pin it back and out of the way.

And she didn't look at him as she forced herself to walk back into the bedroom and pushed her feet into the brand-new spiky-heeled shoes he'd selected to go with the dress.

For if she looked at him he would read the raw and terrifying emotion in her eyes. It was too new, too shattering to be disguised, especially by someone as inexperienced as she knew herself to be.

And what then? Would he take that naked passion, demand it as his right because he, by his own unique alchemy, had brought it into being?

Or would he laugh, contrasting her humdrum ordinariness with what was already his—Helen's gorgeous sexiness, Helen's love—laugh at her because who would drink plain tap water when there was sparkling champagne for the taking?

She couldn't face either scenario and made a great pretence of searching for her handbag, even though she knew where it was and didn't need it anyway, so conscious of him that she thought she might faint.

Watching her move about the room, Luke felt the heat of forbidden desire clutch his loins. The moment he'd seen her at her engagement party he'd felt desperately, achingly sorry for her. A mousy little thing, completely overshadowed by her beautiful, dazzling, irresistible sister.

But she was seemingly content to fade into the wallpaper, because from what he had gathered she'd been brought up that way—the second-born, second-rate sister from whom little was expected. And she was about to be married to a stuffed shirt who would walk all over her, stamp her into the mould he believed he wanted, never allowing her the time or space to find out who she really was, what she wanted from life.

He had determined then to do what he could to open her eyes to her own possibilities. He had teased her, taunted her, pulled her this way and that and, yes, flirted with her, shown her what it was like to be properly kissed, because, despite her involvement with the stuffed shirt, he had known instinctively that she was totally unawakened sexually.

He bunched his hands in the pockets of the narrow black trousers he was wearing, the cream dinner jacket parting over his cream silk shirt, his eyes brooding.

So he'd achieved almost all he'd set out to do. She'd left that going-nowhere job to take one that would stretch her to the limit and she'd been tempted into choosing clothes that would show her to be as attractive in her own way as her vibrant sister.

He could hardly believe the way the black chiffon shift he'd plucked out of her wardrobe enticingly displayed the gorgeous curves that had previously been smothered by hopelessly dowdy stuff, the scooped neckline revealing the creamy skin of her upper breasts, the die-for cleavage that made his fingers itch to explore in loving detail, his mouth ache to suckle the pert globes that were so erotically cradled in filmy fabric, the short hemline showing off legs that were wickedly, slenderly elegant . . .

In a moment, he knew, he'd give in to the gratingly urgent, forbidden need to touch, to rip the dress from her back and kiss her body to full awareness. His plans for her metamorphosis had rebounded with a vengeance. And it had to stop.

'We've kept Chiara waiting long enough,' he said roughly into the silence. 'Shall we go?'

The grating sexiness of his rough-edged voice brought her head up, her eyes locking with his. Air bunched in her lungs. She couldn't breathe, the intensity of her emotions shaking her by the throat.

There was a slight frown between his magnificent, brooding eyes and his sensual mouth was tugged down at the corners. So her mindless messing about, keeping him waiting, had annoyed him. It hurt. And it shouldn't.

'Of course,' she returned spikily. 'Let's go. I'm ravenous.'

And she walked rigidly from the room, every muscle, every bone held stiffly as she fought the slamming awareness of his closeness, desperately holding onto her composure because she knew that if she lost it she would go to pieces.

And everything held, by some miracle it held, until they emerged onto the loggia.

'This is fabulous,' she said crisply, her voice high and brittle.

Golden lanterns illuminated the area. There was a table set for two and the roses cascading over the terrace looked ghostly in the moonlight, scenting the balmy air.

'Guests could dine here if they preferred,' she went on in that cold, hard voice, adding with a dose of sarcasm, 'Of course, I don't know the proximity to the proposed dining area, not having been given the opportunity to see the plans yet, but—'

'What a prickly little thing you are.' He seated himself on the opposite side of the table, his eyes remote. 'You make every comment sound like an accusation. Lighten up, why don't you?'

Bess swallowed. Hard. Perhaps her remarks, the tone of her voice had been too confrontational. But he needn't look as if he actively disliked her! She felt her composure begin to slip, and made a grab for it, coming back snippily, 'Are all Italian men so all-fired arrogant?' She frowned at the glass of Chianti he'd poured for her, her face going tight as his compelling eyes pulled her gaze back to him.

The flickering golden light of the candle in its amber glass bowl was reflected in the dark and smouldering depths. He looked diabolical, a magnet for the dark forces of all that was wickedly exciting, intrinsically wrong, given their circumstances, sinfully reinforcing her deep and forbidden feelings for him. Tears of yearning, of dredging regret, stung the back of her eyes and the hardness of his voice was almost a relief as he answered her question.

'I'm a half-breed, don't forget. I may have my share of thoroughbred Italian arrogance, but I lack the inborn finesse.' His sparsely fleshed, broad shoulders lifted in a careless shrug. 'I am a mongrel. Remember that. Mongrels fight dirty, if they have to.'

He stared at her face, its beauty tight and troubled. He'd fight any way he could to deny this dangerous attraction, he thought suddenly—even replace the growing sexual tension with direct antagonism, if that was what it took.

'Eat,' he commanded coldly. 'Chiara has gone to some trouble and you said you were ravenous.'

Well, she wasn't. She'd lied. And she should be rejoicing because he'd suddenly found he disliked her, had stopped flirting and teasing. And if her presence irritated him enough, became a bore, he'd be only too glad to see the back of her and let her go, tomorrow, after she'd done what she was here to do.

Her thoughts should have comforted her, but didn't. She felt unbearably hurt, her stomach lurching as she stared with glazed eyes at the no doubt delicious helping of thinly sliced ham, olives, tiny sausages and anchovies he had put in front of her.

She forced some of it down, helped by generous sips of the ruby-red wine, then toyed with the next course—bite-sized pieces of tender lamb flavoured with rosemary which Chiara had proudly presented. Eventually she said, because the brooding silence was unbearable and she was sinking beneath the harsh weight of it and any conversation had to be better, 'Do you have many relatives in Italy, apart from your cousin?'

'Droves of them,' he answered curtly, pushing his unfinished food away, impatience in the gesture.

But she persevered, something driving her to get to know as much about him as she could.

'Do you see them often? Were you born in Italy, or in England? Perhaps you have a home of your own here?'

She knew she sounded breathless, but the words suddenly tripping off her tongue were born of a last desperate need to flesh him out.

She would never, she recognised sadly, be able to discuss him with her sister. It would be far too painful. She would do her level best to avoid the couple whenever possible after the wedding, at least until the pain in her heart became more manageable.

'So many questions!' But he sounded more relaxed, as if a conversation centred on his roots was safe territory. He shrugged lightly then gestured over the terrace where, down in the valleys far below, pinpricks of light showed the existence of tiny villages. 'I was born here in Tuscany. It calls to me sometimes. I feel it deep in my heart—a loss, a regret.'

'You'd like to make your home here again?' she guessed, drawn by the yearning note in his honey-dark voice. He told her, 'When the time is right, yes.'

When he and Helen had been married a year or two, were ready to start a family. It made sense. And it hurt. Unbearably. But he was telling her easily, 'By the time I was born in a villa on the banks of the Arno, on the outskirts of Pisa, the family had come a long way from its peasant roots. My father was head of my great-grandfather's merchant bank and had married into an English county family.'

He was looking away as he spoke, avoiding the huge, consuming eyes. He supposed he was talking about his background because it was easier to bear than the earlier taut silence, and the information was harmless enough. 'My mother wasn't happy in Italy and after my father died we lived in London. She has never been back.'

'How old were you when your father died?' Bess was glad he wasn't looking at her. That way she could indulge the desire to devour him with her eyes, study those lean, dark features, the soft, silky fall of his hair, the firm masculine jawline, the cruel yet sensually beautiful mouth, to imprint his image on her mind in guilty secrecy because the image of him was all she would have, the man himself being strictly out of bounds.

Then she dropped her gaze quickly as he turned briefly to look at her, telling her, 'Thirteen. I was sent to an English public school and the only concession made to my Italian heritage at that time was the promise that I should follow in my father's footsteps regarding my career.'

Looking at her had been a huge mistake, he realised. The tension built up massively again. It stung the air. Yet, having turned to her, he couldn't tear his eyes away from the pale oval of her face, framed by that rich, glossy hair, the golden lamp-light making a mystery of her lush lips, smooth, creamy shoulders, stroking, deepening the enticing shadow between her breasts, making the adoring pools of her eyes look fathomless.

Adoring... He groaned silently, cursing himself for what he had done. He had awoken her to her sexual potential, never imagining that all those previously repressed desires would focus on him.

And heaven knew that desire was reciprocated!

It would be fatally easy to do the dishonourable thing. He had to kill the infatuation, for that was all it could be for her, here and now. A muscle jerked at the side of his jaw. It would hurt him as much as it hurt her...

'Anything else you'd like to know?' he asked harshly. 'The size of the shoes I wore when I was ten? When I came out of nappies? When I was weaned?' He drained his wineglass and slapped it down on the table. 'If not, may we end the conversation? It's boring me.'

For a moment she couldn't believe it. The pain round her heart was like nothing she'd ever experienced before. She'd been lulled into softness by the companionable way he'd been talking to her, melting in the atmosphere of secret intimacy, feeling herself drawn closer to him, into him, a part of him, if only for a few magical moments...

'I apologise for boring you,' she managed through cold, wooden lips. There was a giant lump in her throat. Her mouth felt dry.

She stood up, intending to walk away with dignity, but her leg bones had taken a holiday and she couldn't trust herself to move. To stop herself from weeping she informed him, 'Don't blame me if you're used to more sparkling company. You insisted I stay. So be prepared to be bored out of your socks.'

She had to make her exit now. Whatever riposte he cared to make, she wouldn't be able to bear it. She forced herself to move, but her jelly-like legs betrayed her, sending her jerking painfully into the side of the table as she tried to walk around it, and the tiny humiliation was the final straw. The tears she had been so gallantly fighting poured down her face, the sob that had been building in her chest escaping in humiliating disorder.

Her hands came up to cover her face, hiding this final ignominy, and she heard above the rasping of her breath and the uneven pounding of her heart the chink of china as the table was pushed unceremoniously aside.

'*Cara*—don't!' His arms were like steel bands as they came around her. 'I can't take this. I'm sorry. Sorry! Don't cry. Please don't cry.'

His voice was harsh, but not like before; the raw emotion wasn't displeasure, but something else. Something that made her feel light-headed, something that stemmed the flow of tears, sent shudders of wildfire through her veins as his arms tightened, merging their bodies, making her understand that inescapable something and helplessly, eagerly respond.

# CHAPTER SEVEN

THE flash of desire was too intense, too driven to be fought, and Bess wound her arms around his neck, her body beginning to shake.

Luke groaned despairingly as a deep answering shudder raked through his body, and then his mouth took hers and she submitted with mindless willingness to the plundering onslaught, the unstoppable tide of mutual need.

The invasion of his tongue ignited wild explosions throughout her body, creating a fever in her brain, and when the tip of her own tongue instinctively curled around his the conflagration of his untamed response flooded her with a sexual excitement more explicit, more wanton than she had ever dreamed possible.

And as the hard, urgent domination of his arousal thrust against the softness of her belly Bess sank bonelessly against him, transported to a world of winging ecstasy, a kaleidoscope of love in all its glowing facets where nothing existed but her love for him, her need and his.

'Bess!' he uttered hoarsely, a raw expletive thickening his throat as he lifted her bodily in his arms, his mouth returning hungrily to hers as he carried her through the silent building to her room.

And his hands were shaking as he unzipped her dress and slowly slid it from her shoulders, down her body—tiny tremors that added a sense of timeless urgency, made her step lightly out of the pool of fabric and rub the rosy tips of her breasts against his chest, her fingers parting his shirt, needing the touch of his flesh against hers.

Gasping raggedly, he threw back his head, his eyes closed, his mouth a grim rictus as her swollen nipples rubbed against his burning, hair-roughened skin, his whole body tensing for a fragment of time before he dragged her hard against him. His mouth moved feverishly over her skin, her eyelids, the corners of her mouth, the hollows behind her ears and the length of her throat before swooping lower to suckle ardently at the pert, swollen breasts as he had been aching to do since he'd first seen her in that wicked black dress.

As he swept her up in his arms once more and carried her to the bed, the tremors of his hard body matched her own, as if they were already one being. A stab of deep, raw sensation burned with bright savagery in the pit of her stomach when he dragged off his clothing and she saw the satin sheen of his skin, the desperate need in his tarnished-silver eyes, the sheer magnificence of him as he slowly, almost reverently, enclosed her in his arms.

The moment she woke Bess was immediately and sensationally deluged by emotions so deep, so intense that she marvelled that her slight body could contain them without fragmenting into millions of tiny ecstatic pieces.

Without opening her eyes she knew that Luke was still deeply asleep. His breathing was slow and gentle, his naked body warm and vibrant beneath her curving arm.

The temptation to wake him was enormous. Bess resisted. Slowly, carefully, she withdrew her arm and eased herself up on one elbow, and as she looked down at him her heart was wrung with a love that was so intense, it was painful.

He was so beautiful—dark lashes made twin smudgy shadows above his slanting cheekbones and in sleep his lips were parted temptingly. So temptingly...

But, more than that, his passion had been tempered with a gentle consideration, as if he had intuitively known she was a virgin. And as he had entered her, finally, completely, she had breathed his name and he had said thickly, making her feel special, 'Luca. It is my birth name. To you I am Luca.'

And now she asked herself if he had also invited Helen to use the name he had been given before it had been anglicised. The question slammed into her, a physical blow that made her wrap her arms round her body in a futile attempt to contain the shock.

The awful, inescapable, uncontainable shock of guilt.

She had spent the night with her sister's future husband, making love with him time after time, each experience more passionate, more tumultuous, deeper than the one before, her responses to him wildly uninhibited.

It was the ultimate betrayal and she didn't know how she was going to live with herself. Unless— unless he hadn't been able to help himself either, had fallen in love with her as catastrophically as she had with him.

But it needn't be a catastrophe, need it? Not if he had discovered he loved her, not Helen.

She bit down hard on her lower lip, tears flooding her eyes as she realised how much Helen would be hurt. And her mother would never speak to her again. It had been taken for granted that Helen would make a brilliant marriage while she, Bess, would make a sensible one.

Her mother would accuse her of being a thief, stealing her glittering daughter's rightful glory. And Bess had learned early never to try to stand in her sister's limelight, never to expect the best things in life which Helen demanded, and got, as of right.

Closing her eyes, forcing back tears, she knew she had to be sensible about this. And that shouldn't be difficult. She was famous for it, wasn't she?

Her throat closed up. As soon as Luca woke they would talk things through, calmly, like the adults they were. But when he said her name, softly, the possibility of a sensible, rational discussion flew out of the window and she blurted out wildly, 'Luca— I love you—so much it hurts!' Then she turned to him trustingly, her green eyes huge in the pallor of her face, knowing that together, somehow, they would sort this out.

But he didn't move; his body, turned towards her now, was locked in a stillness that was frightening, his features set.

'Luca?'

There was a plaintiveness in her husky voice that made him hate himself. His eyelids flickered, masking his self-disgust. Last night was something he would never forget; her loving had been so precious, so sweet and generous. But he should have had more self-control. She deserved better than a one-night stand or a brief and secret affair.

She deserved fidelity, the lifelong commitment of one man, a commitment of love and caring, not— He blanked out his thoughts and knew he had to force her to see her emotions for what they were. Infatuation. She was on a hiding to nothing; he cared about her enough to want to make her understand that. And there was only one way.

He reached for her, hoisting her back against the pillows, his voice low, the teasing note sounding slightly forced as he told her, 'We'll forget you said that, shall we?' He pinned her hands above her head with one of his own, his eyes brooding darkly as they bored deeply into hers, only the smile that curved his sensual mouth giving her any re-assurance at all.

And that only lasted until he said, 'You don't know what love is, believe me. You were brought up on a diet of stodgy old Tom. What you feel for me is infatuation, I promise. Because, never having known anything like it before, this is what you love.' Then he took each nipple in turn, suckling deeply, making her powerless to say anything, to assure him that she'd loved him before he'd taken her to bed, that sex for the sake of it, mere infatuation, was nothing to do with the way she felt.

'And this,' he continued remorselessly as his hands moved down to her hips, making her body writhe with the need to have him fill her. 'And this—' He slid his hands over the soft swell of her stomach, then further down, brushing with slow sensuality over the tangle of coppery curls, driving her wild. 'This is what you love. Nothing to be ashamed of; it's entirely natural. But don't mistake it for anything else.'

He planted a hard, punishing kiss on her mouth and twisted off the bed, plucking his abandoned clothes off the floor. 'See you for breakfast in half an hour.'

Bess stared at the empty space where he had been, her eyes wide with shock. Then slowly, excruciatingly, her heart squeezed as humiliation filled it.

He had used her—simply and callously used her. He had come into her life and wrecked it, changed her for ever, pulled her out of the safe little world she had contentedly inhabited—a nice, comfortable little world carved from her perceived inadequacies and walled in by the strength of her insecurities—only to plunge her into the hell of loving him, betraying her own sister.

Then anger flooded hotly through her, making her leap from the bed and make the decision to tell him exactly how she felt, what she thought of him—the ratfink!—to explain how easily love could turn to blind hatred, do the job she'd come here to do and get back to England as fast as she could already made.

Defiantly, because she needed to bolster her confidence, keep her own flag flying, she dressed in the flame-red top and matching trousers, piled her coppery curls loosely on top of her head, leaving a few tendrils to frame her face, and marched downstairs, her heart hammering.

Chiara found her in the huge hall and ushered her into a small panelled room. It was as much as Bess could do to return the older woman's friendly smile. Her thoughts were too savage to be deflected by the need for normal politeness.

The dust sheets had been removed from the furniture and everything gleamed, the circular table in the deep window embrasure laid for breakfast. But Bess wouldn't be eating a thing.

Luca was there, his head bent over the papers in his hand, and, even in her hatred, she had to admit that he looked startlingly, temptingly gorgeous in the soft worn denims and loosely styled pale grey silk shirt, open at the neck to reveal a few inches of sexy, hair-roughened olive skin.

As he heard her approach he looked at her, his silver eyes making a slow inventory of her tight-fitting scarlet trousers and the matching sleeveless top with its seductively dipping neckline. And then his face went tight.

'Breakfast first, and then we work,' he said with a cool politeness that added fuel to the fire of her hatred.

She waved aside the mention of breakfast; the very thought of eating made her feel ill. How could he act as if last night hadn't happened, as if she had never told him she loved him? How could he talk to her as if she were a stranger?

'Work suits me.' Her voice was tight with harnessed rage. 'I want to get away from here before nightfall.' Bitterness welled up inside her. 'But before we get down to it I want you to know that I won't tolerate any more insults from you.'

'Insults?' His dark brows bunched. 'When have I insulted you, *cara*?'

'And don't call me that!' The careless endearment was too much to take. 'It's meaningless.'

Her nostrils thinned. 'You insult me every time you look at me the way you do.'

She turned away, staring through the tall window, seeing nothing. There were things that had to be said, but she couldn't bear the scrutiny of those handsome silver eyes.

'I told you how I felt about you and you threw it back in my face, letting me know you consider me a sex-starved fool.' The wobble in her voice was a result of rage—sheer gut-searing rage. It had to be. She forced herself on. 'You treated me like a common whore. And if that's not an insult then I'm a pineapple!'

'Cara—'

She hadn't heard him approach her but she felt his hands as they lightly touched her shoulders and knocked them frenziedly away, spinning round and edging backwards until she was trapped against the window.

'OK.' He spread his hands, making no attempt to crowd her. 'I don't think you're a fool—far from it. As for the rest—' his eyes gleamed narrowly '—I stand by what I said.'

'That all I needed was a man. That any man would have done, given the state of my hormones,' she said flatly, her eyes unconsciously vulnerable, and she shivered suddenly, wrapping her arms defensively around her body. 'Don't try to make me believe I'm down in your dark pit. I'm not. I do have some integrity.'

But not as much as I always believed, she thought hollowly. Not nearly as much. She had been as willing as he to betray Helen.

She heard his heavy sigh but couldn't see his expression through the unwelcome haze of despised tears, shuddering uncontrollably as he bit out harshly, 'Grow up, woman! I've shown you you're capable of being whatever you want to be—practically shoved your beautiful face in your own sensuality. I admit I want you—you excite me more than I'm comfortable with—but that doesn't mean you can expect me to walk through the rest of your life holding your hand!'

He would have walked out then—he had said all he could say—but the pain in her lovely eyes defeated him. He said impulsively, 'Look, I'll lay my cards on the table,' He would have to be honest with her, he realised. After last night he owed it to her to explain why he wasn't able to take the gift of her love.

It was tempting, but to accept it would mean using her. A discreet affair, short or long, wasn't what he wanted for her. She deserved far better. And when she understood that nothing on earth would make him change his plans, fall in love with her, marry her, she would want nothing more to do with him. She was sensible enough to cut her losses, mark it down to experience, and emerge stronger and wiser.

Aware of the darkness in his voice, but unable to do anything about it, he suggested, 'Why don't we sit down and talk it over? Then, when you've had time to digest it all calmly, you can tell me if you still feel the same.'

He had already turned to the table, pushing aside the papers he'd been looking at earlier—which, Bess now saw, were the architects' plans for the proposed hotel—and was pouring coffee for them both, and despite her earlier decision to get out of here as soon as she could, put him and the whole disgraceful episode out of her head, her heart jerked with stupid hope.

Maybe he was going to confess how reluctant he was to hurt Helen. How torn he was. How guilty. Poor Luca—he was going to marry her sister but had fallen in love with her, Bess. Surely he couldn't have made love with such passion and tenderness if he didn't love her? she thought naïvely.

He would be feeling as bad, as guilty as she did, but he was intelligent enough to know that it wouldn't be fair to marry Helen if he loved someone else. It would be hard, but they were in this mess together, and together, somehow, they would sort it out.

He sat as soon as she did, slowly stirring his coffee, and her love for him came surging back, stronger after its brief translation into hate. She wanted to reach out and touch his hand but the grim line of his mouth and the spasmodic jerking of a muscle at the side of his jaw warned her to leave it.

He lifted his eyes to her. They were dark with something that could have been pain, but she couldn't be sure. He gave a hard, tight sigh, then told her, 'I won't pretend I regret what happened last night. How could I? You were exquisite.' Dull colour stroked his slanting cheekbones. 'I was hungry for you. I still am. Nevertheless, it shouldn't have happened. You do know why, don't you?'

His coming marriage to Helen. Of course she knew, and of course she understood what he must be feeling. Under the brooding intensity of his eyes she nodded mutely, her tongue flicking out to moisten her lips, unable to articulate because the look in his eyes, his mention of hunger held her in thrall.

She now knew what it was to hunger.

'We're going to have to talk this through—' He broke off, frowning, the sound of footsteps breaking the quiet morning.

Chiara coming to clear a breakfast that hadn't been touched? Bess wondered. But she didn't think it likely that the comfy Italian housekeeper would be wearing stilettos on duty—if ever.

High heels on the marble floor of the hall produced that rapid, almost excited sound, and Luca turned his head in the direction of the door. Waiting. Waiting.

Bess held her breath, feeling stupidly apprehensive, and expelled it on a sigh of misery, of racking guilt, when the door was flung open and Helen stood there, a picture of golden, glorious sensuality framed in the carved splendour of the ancient doorway.

The ensuing tiny moment of silence was charged with dark, stinging tension until Helen broke it, swooping over the floor, her arms outstretched.

'Surprise, surprise!'

Luca unfolded his elegant length from the chair and was ready when Helen hurled herself into his arms, her body fitting his as if it belonged there as she crooned, 'Pleased to see me, darling? I had to be in Rome—someone to see—I couldn't not come to see you, could I?'

She wriggled closer, the lemon-yellow silk of the dress she was wearing shimmering seductively over her sensually understated curves. 'And I need to discuss arrangements—Mummy and I can't agree. Shall we have the twelve bridesmaids—or would that be overegging the pudding?'

'Whatever you decide on will be fine by me, you know that—or should do. It will be your big day, after all.'

If his voice was wooden, Bess put it down to guilt. That or the teasing proximity of those luscious scarlet lips, the near-impossibility of resisting the kiss that was so obviously expected while the woman he'd spent last night in bed with was hovering in the background.

Whatever, the wedding was clearly going ahead. She stumbled to her feet. She felt violently, physically ill.

Her movement must have alerted the other two to her presence. They'd been too absorbed in each other to spare time to pay any attention to her.

Helen turned her lovely head, staring at Bess as if she didn't know who she was.

Then her delicate eyebrows peaked. 'Goodness, I didn't recognise you. What on earth have you done to yourself?'

She meant the scarlet trousers and top, the high-heeled strappy sandals she'd bought to go with the outfit. Colour flared briefly on Bess's face then died away. The way Helen looked at her, the half-amused, half-exasperated tone of her voice made her feel five years old, dressed up in her mother's clothes.

She was going to have to walk out of here naturally, pretend that her heart wasn't hurting like hell. Trying to summon the courage for what seemed an impossible task, she heard Helen say dismissively, 'You're doing some sort of work for Luke. Tom did tell me. He came over, furious because he'd wanted you back there, visiting with some old aunt or other.' She moved out of the circling arms, wriggling provocatively as she smoothed the heavy silk over her hips. 'God, what a journey—flight from Rome to Pisa then taxi to here. Thought we'd never find this place—the driver had never heard of it, had to look it up on some grubby old map.'

Her eyes glinted at Bess. 'A word of advice, little sister. About Tom. If you insist on stamping around in your career girl's shoes, you're going to lose him. He's not so smitten that he wouldn't look elsewhere. Your holding power was your dependability, your docility.' Her eyes narrowed, flicking over the brave scarlet outfit. 'Let's face it, there's not much else, is there?'

Then her mouth curved irrepressibly. She came as near as Bess had ever heard her to giggling. 'And underneath he's not as stolid as he looks. We actually managed quite an enlightening conversation after I'd soothed him down over the aunt business. Now...' She turned to the silent Italian, her head on one side. 'Give me breakfast, darling, and we'll have our cosy chat—discuss all the exciting arrangements.'

'I'll leave you to it.' Somehow Bess found the strength to move, but her fingers were shaking as she took the plans from the table. 'I'll take these with me,' she said, not looking at either of them.

She heard Luca say her name, his voice hoarse with strain, but continued walking, not turning to respond—she couldn't; she simply couldn't—and closed the door softly behind her, going to her room.

There she forced herself to think exclusively of what she had to do. She had to study the plans, make notes for Mark, add what she hoped would pass for reasoned opinions, pack her bags and scribble a terse note telling Luca she'd seen enough and had left, leaving it with the plans on the now cleared breakfast table.

The place seemed deserted when she left. She would have liked to say goodbye and thank you to Chiara. But she wasn't going to try to find her. She would run the risk of coming across the others and she didn't want to know where they were, what they were doing. She didn't want to have to think of either of them. Ever again.

# CHAPTER EIGHT

'HELLO, Mum. How's everything? Any news?' Bess had been back in London for over three weeks now and this was the first time she'd phoned home. Oh, she'd sent a couple of postcards, just to say hello, explaining that she'd be too busy with her new job to visit for a while. And she'd sent similar hasty scrawls to Tom.

She was uncomfortably aware that she should have told him she couldn't marry him long before now, but she didn't feel able to face any of them just yet. And, thankfully, he hadn't tried to contact her. He was probably still deeply annoyed with her over the issue of the job and his wealthy old aunt.

She listened to her mother go on and on about village affairs—the church fête, the golf club committee, the sub-postmistress's bad back—until finally she cut in and asked what she'd really phoned to find out.

'Is Helen back from Italy yet?'

'Oh, yes—ages ago.' Jessica Ryland gave the tinkling laugh that told Bess she thought she was a fool. 'Of course she is! We're so busy, you wouldn't believe—so much to think about, so much to do!'

'And when's the big day?' Bess had to know. She would make sure Mark sent her out of the country on a job that she could pretend was too vitally important to postpone. She'd do anything, tell any lie to avoid having to watch the man she loved marry her sister.

'So she's told you?' Jessica sounded surprised, and not pleasantly, either. 'It was going to be the world's best kept secret until practically the last minute. She's threatened us all with the direst consequences if we as much as let a word slip to anyone.' Then the huffincss eased a little. 'But yes, she would have felt shc had to tell you. You are her sister, I suppose.'

Welcome to the family! Bess thought drily, wondering if Helen had wanted to keep her wedding plans such a strict secret because she wasn't totally sure of Luca's commitment. Then, her stomach clenching sickeningly, she heard her mother gush on, 'Only another four weeks. You can't think how much there is to arrange—and then rearrange because the dear girl's changed her mind! Still, you can't blame her; it's going to be her big day, after all, so naturally she wants everything to be perfect.

'There's the guest list, of course. It gets longer and longer—but we're going to have to get it off to the printer's soon. Then there's the flowers, the photographers... Your father's doing the sensible thing and keeping well out of it—simply footing the bills—which, so he says, is quite enough!'

All Bess had to do was make suitable murmurs from time to time. And even that was almost beyond her. Stupidly, she had hoped that the wedding was off, that Luca had told Helen that he had fallen in love with someone else. Hoped with stupid desperation, even though she had known in her heart that it wouldn't happen.

But the wedding was obviously going ahead as planned and she knew that if she told her mother, right now, that she had decided not to marry Tom, then Jessica would probably murmur something like, 'How nice,' and burble on about the reception, Helen's dress, the honeymoon.

None of her family would blink at the news of her broken engagement. They would be too busy being happy over the anticipation of the wonderful Helen's brilliant marriage to one of the decade's most eligible men to give a single thought to her.

She had often felt alone in her life, excluded, but this was the first time it had really mattered, and her face was white as she inserted, 'Must go, Mum—there's someone at the door.' Any made-up excuse would do to end this painful, one-sided conversation, and she replaced the receiver and gripped the edges of the table, her face closed up with dredging misery.

'So there you are! I'm going to give myself a facial—want to help?'

Niccy's cheerful voice barely penetrated the fog of despair. Slowly, Bess turned unseeing eyes in the direction of her friend.

Niccy was going out this evening. A new man. They'd known each other for months and suddenly he was showing a decided interest. And Niccy seemed willing to return it. Bess had thought she'd be out of the way for hours, locked in the bathroom making herself gorgeous.

'I'm sorry?' She hadn't properly caught what the other girl had said. She hadn't been listening to anything but the anguish of her heart.

Niccy stopped smiling, her voice serious as she asked, 'Bess, what's wrong?' She moved closer. 'You've been phoning? Bad news?'

'No.' Bess bit her lip. Not bad news, just the worst. But it had been predictable. She tried to smile, but her face was too stiff.

'Tell me what's wrong,' Niccy insisted. 'And don't say "Nothing". Since you came back from Italy you've looked as if you can't think of one good reason for living. Except work. You never stop. And you've lost weight—which isn't surprising,' she tacked on sternly, 'since you barely eat a thing. So tell me; it might help.'

She wrapped her thin arms round Bess impulsively, comforting her, and that was her undoing. The tears came, pouring unheeded down her cheeks as she raggedly confessed, 'I've been such a fool. And worse. I hate myself!'

And while Niccy led her into the sitting room and steered her onto the sofa it all came pouring out. Everything. She held nothing back, punishing herself, and, strangely enough, she did feel relief of a kind, as if it was easier to come to terms with her own true feelings when they were spoken aloud.

'Drink this.' Niccy had poured a generous measure of fine old brandy into a glass and she pushed it into Bess's hand.

'I think I really hate him,' Bess stated. 'I must do, mustn't I?' She stared into the amber liquid. It was early evening and she hadn't eaten all day—at least she didn't think she had—and it would go straight to her head; she knew it would.

'That doesn't surprise me,' Niccy put in heatedly. 'He sounds like a prize rat!'

Bess hunched her shoulders. 'I guess he's one of those men with an over-active libido. Perhaps he can't help it—else why would he bother with me when he's about to marry Helen? She's so lovely. But he's a sensual animal and I was available—and more than willing. So he used me.' She took a sip of the potent liquid. 'When I told him I loved him he thought it was a joke. He explained quite graphically what it really was—in his cynical opinion. Just sex. Not that he was complaining.'

She twisted the glass round, swirling the brandy, and took a reckless swallow, welcoming the warmth that curled right through her because she hadn't felt warm inside since... 'He'd have probably taken me to bed every night I was there, and I'd have let him because I was in love with him, blinded by it,' she admitted with painful honesty. 'Only Helen turned up. And that's what's giving me nightmares.'

'Guilt?' Niccy guessed. 'Oh, you poor thing. And what about Tom? Will you tell him?'

Bess gave her friend a blank look then shook her head slowly.

'About what happened? No. I can't marry him, of course, but I won't tell him about Luca—Luke,' she corrected, vowing never again to even think about him in connection with the name he had asked her to use. That name belonged to fantasy, to a wild romance beneath the velvet Tuscan sky. This was the bleak reality.

'He might go straight to Helen and tell her,' she explained. 'He can't stand the sight of her, and telling her that her husband-to-be can't be faithful for two minutes would probably be justified in his opinion. It would take her down a peg or two, which is something he's always said she needs. And what I can't decide is whether to tell her or not.'

Giving her friend an anguished look, she asked, 'What do you think? If he's unprincipled enough to give in to his insatiable sex-drive, to make love to his future sister in-law just weeks before his wedding, just think what her life will be like—she'll never know where he is or what he's doing and who he's doing it with! It would be a terrible thing to do, but—'

'Say nothing,' Niccy advised emphatically. 'It would be pointless. She'd hate you for the rest of her life—naturally. And my guess is the wedding would go ahead regardless. Financially, socially and in the looks department, Luke Vaccari's one hell of a catch. Helen wouldn't let him slip through her greedy fingers because of what she would convince herself was a minor indiscretion. She'd make herself believe it was all your fault.

'My advice is to leave them alone to get on with their own lives. And you get on with yours. You're not the first girl to fall for a rat and you won't be the last.' Her voice softened. 'Are you sure about Tom? You seemed so certain he was the right man for you. Maybe when you're over the episode with Vaccari you'll regret breaking up with Tom. Couldn't you explain, ask him to give you time—?'

'No,' Bess said decisively. It would take her a long time to recover from having fallen in love, really, deeply in love, for the first time. It wasn't, as Niccy seemed to think, something she'd forget in a month or two, put behind her.

'One thing he did do for me,' she revealed quietly, 'was change me. He made me see that life is full of endless possibilities. He opened things up for me. So much so that I couldn't marry Tom now even if I'd never fallen for Luke. I can't spend the rest of my life being what Tom and my parents—my mother particularly—expect me to be: dutiful, quiet, uncomplaining...

'Now look.' She got to her feet, wobbled a bit, blamed the brandy, and chivvied, 'You'll be late for your date if you don't get a move on. And thanks for listening, for making me talk. It has helped, honestly.'

Helped in the context that it had made her see that life had to go on, she mused the next morning. She'd even forced herself to eat a proper breakfast before leaving for work, and made herself take a renewed interest in her appearance. Thus she was wearing her favourite suit—a neat navy skirt topped by a fitted white jacket which thrust her riot of copper curls to vivid prominence, deepened the colour of her green, green eyes and emphasised the sultry curve of her coral mouth.

So far, so good. But she would never forget him, she thought as she switched on her word processor. Never. That brief interlude of forbidden passion would always be there, right in the centre of her heart.

Tightening her lips, she began to work, and when Mark walked into her office she was deep in projected costings and barely spared him a glance until he told her, 'You have the afternoon off. Luke Vaccari phoned me at home last night. He said your discussion might take some time, hence the elastic lunch-hour.'

He wandered over and stared at the screen. 'It's got to be something to do with his cousin's place, so make sure you take the relevant notes with you.' He backed off, already leaving. 'If it was anything to do with the finance package he'd have asked for me.'

For a panicky, dizzying moment she was tempted to run after Mark and beg him to go in her place. She actually sprang to her feet, but common sense put her back on her seat again.

Her boss would think she'd flipped, and, much as the thought of meeting Luke again sent her haywire, the sensible part of her brain told her that this might be the only opportunity she would ever get to warn him against the kind of promiscuous behaviour that would hurt her sister, ruin their marriage.

For, even though she'd always been in awe of her glittering sister, afraid of her sharp tongue, she did love her, and wanted her to be happy.

Forcing herself to concentrate, she grimly got on with the job in hand, but as one o'clock approached she was fluttering inside. Would she be able to handle this? Would she be able to cope with the way she felt about him?

She renewed her lipstick with shaky fingers and walked through to the front office. He was waiting and she knew immediately that nothing could, or ever would, make her immune to the sheer impact of him.

Tall, he had that lithe, lean grace which enabled him to wear beautifully tailored clothes to perfection, a forbidding grace that sent shudders tumbling down her spine, culminating in a shock of raw sensation deep in the core of her body. And his face, beneath the fall of perfectly cut soft dark hair, was something to die for, every woman's secret fantasy.

Bess swallowed convulsively, clenching her hands around her briefcase. Unsmiling, his silver eyes held hers with an intensity that was frightening and she said thickly, her mouth feeling numb, 'I'm ready if you are.'

'Of course.'

His eyes still held hers, his mouth tight, and she looked away quickly because that level of intensity was making her more than nervous. She walked to the door. There was a cab waiting, and to make sure that the initial part of the meeting was kept strictly to business she told him coolly, 'I put my thoughts on your cousin's hotel plans down on paper and, after talking it over with Mark, added a few suggestions. It's all here.'

She patted her briefcase, refusing to look at him. 'Everything could have been sent through the post—there was no need for a meeting. But you can tell her the project looks promising from Jenson's point of view.'

'There's every need for a meeting,' he told her tersely. 'And it has nothing to do with Emilia's plans.'

And no prizes for guessing what was on his mind, she thought miserably. He was going to ask her to keep silent about their night of passion. He had been indiscreet. He wouldn't want Helen to find out.

She wondered sickly what inducement he might think fit to offer. Or would he use threats?

Whatever, she wished herself a whole galaxy away from where she was—so closely confined with the man she couldn't stop loving, yet so far from him in every way that really mattered. She experienced a wave of relief when the brief journey was over, only to tense right up again as he escorted her into the restaurant he'd chosen.

It was obviously expensive, the tastefully set tables far enough apart for privacy, the atmosphere hushed, almost reverent, a temple for the enjoyment of good food and wines, sophisticated conversation.

'Shall I order for you?' Silvery eyes lifted from the leather-bound menu in his strong, lean hands, noting that hers lay unopened on the damask-covered table.

Bess nodded. She didn't want to be here. She didn't know if she could handle this. Maybe she should just say her piece and get up and go.

But she didn't move and within moments he was giving their order and her wineglass was filled. She stared at it blankly, not daring to look at him, not wanting to hear him demand her silence, dismiss what had been between them as an unimportant folly, not worth causing a scene between him and his intended wife. Not worth a row of beans.

'Bess. Look at me, Bess.'

She couldn't. She sensed his brittle mood keenly. It cut her like a knife because she knew the reason for it. But after a few moments she made herself look at him, lifting her head proudly, glittering green eyes holding silver ones darkened to brooding grey.

'Don't worry. I won't say a word to anyone about what happened.' Niccy would never repeat what she'd been told. Bess could trust her with her life. And she dropped her eyes as a plate was deftly put in front of her.

Beautifully served scallops. No doubt delicious but she wouldn't be eating. She'd just give him the papers, issue the warning about two-timing Helen after their marriage—the one she'd been rehearsing in her mind—and leave.

She raised her eyes to his again and he said thickly, 'Bess—don't!'

The sudden bleak shaft of pain she saw beneath the furrowed brows sent her into shock; she was immobilised by the intensity of what he was revealing. He reached for her hand across the table, his fingers winding with possessive savagery around hers.

'I can't believe how much I've missed you!' His voice was raw.

He had fought it—God, how he had fought it, he mused. Told himself a thousand times that the madness was over. Finished. Ended. But it wasn't over. Perhaps it never would be.

When Helen had walked in on them he had been about to tell her the cold, basic facts, open his heart, let her make the choice. Whatever happened or didn't happen between them in the future would be her decision.

At first he had cursed the unlooked-for interruption, but later, when he'd discovered that she'd hightailed back to England, he'd remembered his priorities and counted Helen's unexpected arrival as a blessing. Helen had unwittingly saved him from making a bad mistake.

But now, after weeks of listening to his conscience, telling himself that he knew what was right for her—and an affair with him wasn't that—he found he couldn't help himself.

Mistake or not, he had to tell her what he wanted. He was driven by the need. And, although she'd been defensive, prickly, distant, now that he touched her he knew it wasn't over for her, either.

Knew it by the way she returned the biting pressure of his fingers, the rapid movement of her gorgeous breasts as they rose and fell beneath the smooth white jacket, by the sudden delicate flush of rosy colour on her cheeks, the way her soft lips parted, her eyes closing to mask the haze of desire he'd so briefly yet unmistakably glimpsed in those shimmering deep green depths.

Food forgotten, he lifted her hand to his lips, smothering the slender fingers with feather-light kisses, and saw her face go white, her mouth twist with pain as if she'd been dealt a mortal blow.

Bess dragged her hand away from the drugging pleasure of his lips, reality sending her hurtling into cold despair. He only had to touch her to make her lose all sense of decency, a helpless victim of her tortured needs.

'Don't do this to me,' she pleaded thinly, sitting very upright, very rigid, consciously holding herself together because she was desperately afraid of going to pieces. 'You make me hate myself.'

'Why?' He looked at the end of his tether, his patience only kept by an immense effort of will. 'Is

the way we feel about each other—wanting each
other—something to be ashamed of?'

She dragged a sharp breath through her nostrils.
'You won't defeat me with that kind of logic,' she
told him rawly. 'You disgust me almost as much as
I disgust myself. I can't stop you cheating on Helen
in the future, but it won't be with me.' She glared
into his frowning eyes, recognising the question
mark in the silver depths. 'Never again. Marry her,
if that's what you want. But I never want to have
to see you again.'

# CHAPTER NINE

'THIS is intolerable!'

Even though Bess had already made a move to leave he was on his feet before her. Their waiter came gliding up immediately, as if he were on supersonic castors, and Bess, willing her legs to stop shaking, waited for the small moments it took for Luke to assure the anxious man that there was nothing wrong with the food or the ambience, apologise, settle the bill in full and sweep her out, only the inescapable grip of his hand on her arm keeping her upright.

Thankfully, a taxi had just drawn up, disgorging elegantly dressed passengers who disappeared into the restaurant, talking together in low voices. Bess, hovering between plain old-fashioned hysteria and gut-wrenching misery, hoped these people would stay long enough to eat the meal they ordered.

Wrenching free, she darted forward and gave the office address to the driver.

'Cancel that,' Luke instructed bitingly from right behind her, hustling her inside and naming a street in Little Venice.

'I don't want—' she spat out contemptuously, but he cut her off, turning to her as the vehicle drew out into the traffic, his eyes glittering darkly.

'At this moment I don't give a damn what you want—or think you want. What I need, what we both need, is a little time, a little privacy.' He settled

back in his seat, giving her a look that dared her
to argue. 'You've obviously got a few wires crossed.
And we're going to have to straighten them out.'
He angled himself into the corner, pinning her with
his eyes. 'To begin with, what gave you the idea I
wanted to marry Helen? I have no intention of
doing any such thing, believe me.'

'Does she know that?' she snapped at him. Who
did he think he was lying to? She knew what she
knew, didn't she? Only last night her mother had
been going on about the logistics of preparing for
a glittering wedding!

'I would imagine the thought has never entered
her head,' he responded, almost lightly. 'And when
we arrive at my home you can tell me why it entered yours. And while we're getting there try to
relax; take a few deep breaths. I don't make love
to unconscious women, and you look about to pass
out.'

She wanted to tell him he wasn't funny, that
lovemaking—oh, heaven forbid!—wasn't something to make jokes about. But she did feel peculiar;
she could almost feel the pallor in her face. She
pressed her fingers to her eyes and began to shake.
Was he telling the truth, or just being unspeakably
cruel?

The breeze from the canal revived her as they
reached their destination and exited the cab. It
feathered through her hair and trickled over her
skin, cooling her.

'This is where you live?' she asked, simply for
something to say. She couldn't yet bring herself to
grapple with the implications of what he'd told her

on the journey. She needed a little more time to get her head straight.

He looked around him, as if surprised by her question, his glance encompassing the quiet, tree-lined street, the stately, white painted mini-mansion which faced the Regent's Canal, magnolias in full bloom, willows bending gracefully over the water, black swans and colourful barges. He shrugged.

'Little Venice. When I am in London, yes, this is where I live.' He took her arm, glancing down at her. 'It's a place to be. Well-mannered. My mother approves of my London address, if nothing else.' His mouth twisted wryly. 'For myself, I would prefer...'

He allowed his preferences to hang on the air, as if for the moment they were unimportant. And as he escorted her towards the porticoed entrance Bess supplied 'Tuscany' in her mind—a word which immediately conjured up images of villages perched on the top of cypress-covered hills, old terraced olive groves disappearing into the hot, shimmering blue haze, craggy mountaintops where the warm wind carried the scent of a thousand herbs.

Horribly, she wanted to cry. She knew so much about this complicated man, and yet she knew so very little. Almost nothing.

'Fortunately, it's my housekeeper's day off. We'll have all the privacy we need,' he told her as he opened the panelled front door. Wordlessly, he swept her through the dignified entrance hall, pushing open a door and standing back for her to enter.

Bess shuddered. She didn't think privacy was a good idea where she and this man were concerned.

She looked round the room with awe. Furnished with restrained elegance, it had massive French windows which opened onto a terrace above a sweep of closely manicured lawn which, in turn, was surrounded by tall trees.

A silent, secluded place. She gave another involuntary shudder, watching as he restlessly paced the gleaming parquet, scuffing up a rug that looked priceless, loosening his navy silk tie with one hand, opening the French windows with the other.

'Outside, in the sun,' he commanded tersely, shrugging out of his suit jacket and draping it casually, along with his tie, over the back of a chair, then extending his hand towards her.

She ignored it, her heart hammering painfully as she demanded, 'Were you telling the truth? Are you trying to tell me you won't be marrying my sister?'

'Outside,' he repeated, but this time there was a smile in his eyes. 'You get the most extraordinary ideas.' He walked out onto the terrace. Bess followed as if pulled by an invisible string. Was he lying? Or what? And what would be the point of lying if the truth were to be made very public indeed in a matter of weeks?

'Why should I be marrying Helen? Admittedly, she's a beautiful creature, and sparkling company, but I've been down that road once, and I've no intention of going down it again. Shall we sit?'

A group of padded loungers were angled around a low table at the far end of the terrace, and as she made her way towards them she noted the profusion of flowering geraniums in white stone containers. Was their strong, spicy scent responsible for the wave of giddiness that washed over her, or was it simply confusion, the sudden washing away of guilt, the sudden hope—?

She smacked that down.

'Everyone knows you and Helen are to marry— in four weeks' time,' she told him thickly, needing to hear him contradict her again because what he had told her, emphatically told her, didn't make sense.

'Name one person,' he challenged, lounging back, a flicker of a smile playing over his mouth, the glint in his eyes positively lethal.

No one had ever come out and told her, not in so many words—but then Jessica had said it was supposed to be a huge secret.

'She has never, ever taken a man-friend home to introduce him to the family,' she defended. 'Let alone invited one to stay for the weekend.' That was ·what had started wedding bells clanging in Jessica's head.

'And she's not working. Apart from a couple of trips to London, apparently, and the short trip to Italy, she's been living at home since the weekend you spent there with her. And that's unheard of. Since she landed her first assignment her career's meant more than anything to her. Getting her to relax, take a breather, was always impossible. Yet it's been weeks—'

'On that flimsy evidence you decided she was to be the second Mrs Luke Vaccari?' he scorned, and put like that it did sound stupid.

But Bess rose to the occasion, pointing out, 'You told me yourself she was busy choosing a wedding dress—weeks ago. And I heard her ask you if twelve bridesmaids would be over the top. You told her

you didn't mind—it would be her big day, after all.
And only last night I was talking to Mum—she told
me how busy she and Helen were—ordering
flowers, finalising the guest list—that sort of stuff.'

How could he deny the facts? She dropped her
head in her hands. What was wrong with her? How
could she love a man who was not only promiscuous but also an unprincipled liar? She'd
thought she knew herself, but patently she didn't.

'Poor baby!' She felt his hands on her arms,
pulling her to her feet. 'I can see how the misunderstanding must have happened. You must have
felt so guilty—making love with the man you believed was about to marry your sister. And what
kind of louse would it have made me seem?'

She heard the gentle regret in his voice. It
sounded so genuine that she was stunned, unable
to resist when he eased her back onto the seat. He
sat on the table in front of her, and she dragged
her gaze from the warmth of his eyes because he
was making her melt inside, willing to believe anything he said, and she mustn't let herself be that
foolish.

'We have to get this out of the way, put your
mind at rest before we can move on,' he told her,
and she didn't have time to examine what he meant
by moving on because he was explaining, 'As for
my relationship with Helen, well, it was the usual
sort of thing. We were introduced at a promotional
party. My company financed the development of
the product and Helen was there as the face that
dominated the advertising campaigns. And, as she'd
be the first to point out, she can be utterly be-
witching, totally irresistible when she wants to be.

'Don't—' He raised his hand to ease away the frown of sharp distaste that had gathered between her eyes, and there was an edge to his honey-dark voice now. 'These things happen.' He sucked in a sharp breath. 'God, you're such an innocent! So innocent it hurts.'

She twisted her head away, her frown deepening. She had lost what innocence she'd had. He had seen to that.

'That tells me nothing,' she said thinly. 'Simply explains your initial relationship.' But did it? Had he and Helen been lovers? It sounded very much like it. 'These things happen,' he had said. And Helen's attitude towards him had been definitely proprietorial.

He ignored her waspish retort and continued steadily. 'She wanted my financial backing and set out to convince me of the viability of her project. She has savings of her own, and your father's willing to help out. But she needed more to get the business off to a flying start.

'Wisely, she's making a career change before she has one foisted on her—bowing out gracefully while she's still on top. A wedding boutique in Mayfair— she aims to sell designs by Europe's newest young talents. Not only bridal gowns but accessories, and bridesmaids' dresses, designer labels for the mother of the bride.

'It's due to open in around four weeks, and she's making a big event of it. There's going to be a catwalk show—hence her question about the number of bridesmaids' dresses to be modelled— plus a champagne reception for invited names, photographers, journalists—the lot. The organ-

ising of which is what is probably tying her and
your mother up in knots right now.

'I accepted her invitation that weekend because
it seemed as good an opportunity as any to talk
business not only with Helen but also with your
father, and when I left the women were up to their
ears in design portfolios.'

His heart jerked as he saw the sudden flare of
joy in her eyes, but there was more to tell her, a
whole lot more. But first...

'You're not wearing your ring.' His mouth curved
slightly but his eyes were serious. 'Lost it again?'

'I—' Bess ran her tongue over his lips. That smile
of his made her feel as if she'd been run over by a
bus, her stomach behaving as if she were on a giant
roller coaster ride, nerves fluttering, pulses racing,
everything inside her going haywire because she
knew the truth now, and he'd said he'd missed her,
and they were free to see if they had something to
build on. 'I can't marry Tom.'

'How did he take it?' She didn't seem too sure
of her decision. Her hesitation told him that.

And his suspicion was confirmed when she
answered quickly, 'I haven't broken the news yet.'
Then, suddenly, she said decisively, 'I'll go to see
him on Sunday. Give him back his ring.'

'Good,' he said heavily. His eyes were bleak and
Bess, unhappy, puzzled at the change of mood,
asked quickly, 'What's wrong?'

'I want to make love to you, that's what's wrong.'
He levered himself to his feet. His face was set. 'So
much so, I don't know if I can handle it.'

'You could before,' she reminded him unsteadily, and saw his eyes close briefly, his lips clamp together, before he gave her a hard, dark look.

'That shouldn't have happened. I'm not proud of it. But it seems,' he added drily, 'I have precious little control where you're concerned. The life you had led, your vulnerability—your very innocence—put you out of bounds. Or should have done. The blame for what happened that night is entirely mine.'

'I don't understand,' she said firmly. She had to be firm or she would go to pieces. Would she ever understand this man?

'You will.' He faced her squarely. 'When I tell you what I've got in mind, you'll understand. And that's what I'm afraid of,' he said tightly. He swung away. 'Neither of us ate lunch. I'll find something—a little food, a little wine.'

He had no desire to eat, but he'd try anything to defuse the situation. It was explosive. He wanted her so badly. Memories of how they'd been together had been driving him wild for weeks.

'I'm not hungry.' Or only for him, she added silently. And desperate to clear the confusion from her mind. He'd dispelled her belief that he and Helen were to marry with a few words of explanation, wiped away the guilt she'd been burdened with for weeks, and that on its own was enough to scramble her brain.

But the way he was acting, almost as if he disliked her, hinting at something unimaginable, confessing that he was disgusted with himself for what had happened that night, was unendurable.

She couldn't take much more, and didn't know why he'd brought her here, if that was the way he felt.

'If you have something to say to me, say it. Then I'll leave. You obviously regret bringing me here.'

'Leave?' Hard hands cupped her face, the burning intensity of his eyes daring her to look away. 'You haunt my mind, torment me!' he said explosively. 'You don't walk away from me, not ever again!'

Then, just as quickly, he released her, gathering control, his eyes self-mocking as he invited, 'Sit down. This might take some time.' He watched her as she sank back on the lounger. She was so beautiful, she took his breath away. Hers was not the brittle, glittering beauty of her sister but a love-liness that went soul-deep.

And what he had to say to her was brutal. And yet he couldn't deny it. He didn't like himself right now.

'Bess...' He wasn't going to dress this up. 'I want you, and I know you want me. We were, very briefly, lovers. It wasn't something we went into lightly—for both of us, for different reasons, it was anguished, driven by a passion, a need neither of us could deny.'

'Lovers...' She picked the word out and examined it nervously. The love had been—still was—all on her side. He'd put what had happened between them down on the level of lust.

He sat down on the low table, leaning forward slightly, his hands hanging loosely between his legs. 'Yes, lovers. And I'd like that to continue. For you, the objections seem to be out of the way. You no

longer want to marry Tom—at least that's what
you're saying now—and you know my relationship
with Helen is purely business. But mine—' he
spread his hands then relaxed them again '—still
exist. It is for you to tell me they're valid. Or not.
Whatever you decide.'

'And they are?' Suddenly she felt afraid. Afraid
of the depth of her passion for this man, a depth
she could so easily drown in. Afraid of the most
clinical way he had told her he wanted her.

He didn't answer her directly, telling her instead,
'I sympathised with you before I met you. Helen
was too engrossed in herself to talk much about her
family, but when she did it was of your parents,
and with affection. You she dismissed. I wonder if
she knew you could be more desirable than she?
That, once awakened to your true potential as a
woman, you would eclipse her? Did she dance at
your engagement party because once you were
safely married to the estimable Tom she knew you
would never be awakened, never threaten her?

'Whatever—' he gave her a wry smile '—when I
saw you, I saw waste. And set out to do something
about it. I meddled—which, believe it or not, is
something I've never felt the need to do before. And
succeeded too well. I watched you, saw the trans-
formation, and wanted you like hell. And, despite
telling myself you deserve better than an affair, that
is what I'm offering you.'

He heard the sudden intake of her breath and
held her eyes with his grim determination to force
her to understand.

'I want you. But I won't denigrate our passion,
our needs by having a hole-and-corner affair.' His

nostrils flared with distaste. 'Having you phone me
when your flatmate's out, or you sneaking over here
on my housekeeper's day off, the odd snatched
weekend at some anonymous hotel.'

His silver eyes bored sharply into the green depths
of hers. 'Do you understand? I can offer you no
long-term commitment, no guarantees, but I want
you to move in here with me, live with me openly.
I will not have either of us act as if our needs are
something to be ashamed of.

'And one thing more. I'm not offering marriage—now or in the future. I know that sounds
brutal,' he said coolly, watching the colour come
and go on her delicate skin, hating himself for what
his need for her was making him do. 'But it's better
to face the facts. If I marry—and I suppose I must,
somewhere down the line—the purpose will be to
get an heir. The sole purpose. I have been as honest
with you as I can be. Now it's for you to decide.'

He stood up, his face austere, and Bess, something withering inside her, shrivelled by what he had
just told her, pointed out tartly, 'I'm good enough
to take to bed, but not good enough to be the
mother of your children! Is that what you're
saying?' Her voice rose raggedly. 'I'm perfectly
capable of providing you with an heir—a whole
clutch of them if that's what you want—so it must
be, mustn't it?'

'Bess—*cara*—' Pain darkened his eyes—a fleeting
display of emotion, quickly controlled. 'I don't
doubt your fertility. But you need—deserve—more
from life than that. Would you want to walk
through your life knowing you'd been married

to provide children—like a brood mare? Think about it.'

The things he'd said had been unbelievably harsh but his voice was achingly gentle as he told her, 'I'll rustle up something to eat now, let you think it over in peace. And Bess . . .' He hesitated as he made to walk back to the house. 'Take your time. Be very sure of what you want.'

She sagged weakly back against the soft cushions, her head throbbing. She knew what she wanted.

She wanted him. His love. For ever. But there was no guarantee of ever obtaining that love, earning it. Just the opposite. He'd been brutally honest with her—did he have any idea how much it had hurt?

She wondered feverishly if she should cut and run—now, while she still had some strength of mind left—or whether she should stay, bowing to the inevitability of her love for him, his excruciating power over her.

She shifted uneasily on the lounger, the sun heating her skin through the thin fabric of her suit. She was walking in a minefield; whether she accepted his offer or not the results would be cataclysmic.

She could move in with him, love him, wake up each morning wondering whether today was the day when he would tell her the affair was over. That he had decided the time was right for marriage—to some well-pedigreed woman who would see nothing unacceptable or even slightly unreal about marrying into a dynasty to provide it with an heir for the future.

Or she could walk away and spend the rest of her life aching for him, regretting . . .

She had no defences against him, that was the problem. She had to fight both him and herself, and had nothing to fight with.

Her lips compressed. She would find something to fight him with. She had to.

# CHAPTER TEN

'FOR how long would your proposed arrangement last?' Bess's bluntness was down to the stiffening she'd forced into her backbone—a weapon to use against the sheer temptation of him.

She watched him put the heavy tray down on the table and tacked on coldly, 'It would be more convenient if I knew what sort of time limit I was looking at. A month? A year?' She couldn't help the note of sarcasm; she wasn't prepared to pussyfoot around this thing. She wasn't used to being propositioned. And the knowledge that he would enter their relationship so objectively, the decision already made to end it when it suited him, was pulling her apart.

She wanted him to love her, but he couldn't. Was he incapable of loving anyone? Or was she, as far as he was concerned, fanciable but unlovable?

One brow was slightly raised in an otherwise blank and beautiful face as he perched on the other lounger; it told her quite plainly that he considered her attitude gauche to the point of rudeness.

Well, that was too bad, she decided raggedly, watching his elegantly made hands as he leant forward and forked wafer-thin slices of cold roast pheasant and tangy pasta salad onto a fine bone-china plate.

The desperately unsettling thing, though, was the way knowing him, loving him, had changed her. If anyone had put such a proposition to her before she would have blushed to the roots of her primly scraped-back hair and slapped his face—all outraged virginity and rigid principles.

Yet here she was, actually discussing his invitation—or trying to, because so far he hadn't said a thing. Falling in love with him had changed her out of all recognition.

But he still wasn't saying anything. He handed her the plate and a huge linen napkin to spread over her knees and there was a grim look in his eyes when he eventually said, 'Why be difficult, Bess? Relax, why don't you? Eat first, and then we can discuss our future. If we're to have a future together, that is.'

He had brought, she saw, champagne on ice, and her throat closed up as she watched him neatly strip the foil from the top of the bottle.

Difficult? She was entitled to be difficult, wasn't she? It wasn't every day the man she loved asked her to be his live-in lady! Offered her paradise with one hand and the certainty that she'd be booted right out of it with the other!

The man she loved. That was the true difficulty. Bess put her plate down on the table. The food would choke her. There was a steel band round her heart and it was tightening by the second, suffocating her.

She loved him to the point of lunacy, so why, she asked herself, wasn't she snatching at the opportunity of living with him? She could work hard at making herself indispensable, couldn't she? Insinuate herself into his heart, teach him to love her, make sure he couldn't live without her.

She could accept his offer as a wonderful, once-in-a-lifetime opportunity. A challenge. Couldn't she?

She saw the danger just in time, and put the brakes on the helter-skelter of her imagination, stopping herself from losing herself completely in the fantasy her mind was creating for her.

'Future? What future do we have? That's what I'm asking.' She balled up her napkin and tossed it on the table where it landed on her unwanted food. 'Discuss it now. What's the point in waiting?'

Why draw out the agony of not knowing what he had in mind? she asked herself. Could he see his need for her body lasting longer than a few short months? She couldn't, not with the track record Mark had told her about. How long ago that seemed. And yet it was a matter of a few weeks only. How rapid, and catastrophic, the change in her had been.

Wordlessly, he gave her a glass of champagne. She barely noticed it. He leaned back, seemingly relaxed, his plate beside hers on the table, also untouched. So he'd lost his appetite too. Because she was being 'difficult'? Because she wasn't already on her way, eager to pack her bags and move in with him?

'Why so confrontational, Bess?' His steely eyes were narrowed, watching her minutely, waiting for her reaction. 'Nervous?'

Nervous? She was gutted with nerves. Her future happiness was on the line here. He held it in his cool, careless hands. Suddenly, perspiration stood in beads on her forehead. Recklessly, she emptied her glass in one long swallow and, twisting the slender stem between her fingers, muttered, 'No. Curious. As I have every right to be.'

'Ah.' He gave her a thin smile, put his barely touched glass down on the table and leaned forward, his silver eyes raking her pale features. 'You know what curiosity did to the cat. Well, we might be killing two cats with one throw, but we'll have to risk that.'

He looked so tired, she thought emotionally. Quite suddenly, he looked exhausted. Contrarily, she now wished she hadn't been difficult and confrontational. She hated to see him looking this way.

'You insist on knowing how long I see our proposed relationship lasting?' he questioned. He spoke slowly, as if he was weighing every word, his eyes holding hers intently. 'How can I give you an answer when there isn't one to give? I made a mistake once before and don't intend to repeat it. I made vows in church, committed my life to Elaine and expected for ever.' Briefly, succinctly, he spread his hands. 'If the experience taught me one valuable lesson, it was that nothing lasts for ever.'

'Do you want to tell me what happened?' she asked into the stretching, straining silence of the warm afternoon air. He had sounded so cynical, so drained.

He must have been badly hurt. Suddenly, sympathy took over, driving her past the barrier of jealousy, the knife-twisting pain of knowing that there had once been a woman capable of igniting his love, his passion, his loyalty. A woman he had loved so deeply that, in losing her, he'd lost the ability to love again.

He shrugged, his eyes going dark. But there was no bitterness in his voice, merely resignation, as he told her, 'I guess you do have a right to know. If only to help you understand the way I am. You see, Bess, I was made a fool of, taken for a ride. And OK, I'm not the first man that's happened to and, like anyone else, I could have come to terms with it.'

He lifted his wide shoulders again, explaining, 'We'd been married only two years when the company got into trouble. Big trouble. One of my uncles—Carlo—had gambled investors' money on the stock market and made spectacular losses. For a time it was thought the whole shooting-match would go under.

'Elaine obviously took the scaremongering in the Press more seriously than my assurances that we'd survive it. She cleaned me out—emptied every joint account we had—and disappeared.' He lanced her a grim look and there was entrenched bitterness in his voice now, a depth of pain that shook her. 'She was pregnant at the time. I later learned she'd had the child aborted. That's what really hurt. Not losing her, not knowing she thought more of my money than she did of me, but losing the child.

'By the time she left the marriage was already beginning to deteriorate, but I would never have left her, never knowingly hurt her. I'd made my vows, committed myself to her, and as far as I was concerned there was no going back on that. And by God, Bess, I had wanted that child!'

The raw pain in his voice touched her as nothing else could have. She only knew he was hurting, that she loved him and must help him, offer comfort if she could. She slid to her feet, kneeling in front of him, taking his hands between hers.

'Oh, Luca—what an evil bitch she must have been! How could anyone do something so wicked?' No wonder he was so wary of making a permanent commitment again, of giving another woman the power to hurt him that much, she thought. And if he did—some years down the road—it would merely be to replace the child he had lost.

But now it didn't seem important. Now she understood. Her heart was wrenched with loving compassion for what his wretched ex-wife must have put him through, for the damage she had done, for the emotional scars she had so selfishly inflicted.

Her huge eyes filled with tears. One of them escaped and fell onto his hand, and that brought him back to her, his head lifting, the carapace of bitterness leaving his eyes, letting him see her again.

He said softly, 'Don't weep for me, *cara*. It all happened a long time ago. I was much younger then, less cynical, less able to protect myself from that kind of hurt. I've moved on, believe me.'

He reached down, clamped his hands around her waist and lifted her onto his lap. And his voice was thick as he told her, 'I never talk about the past, and rarely think of the way she callously killed my child, but you wanted to know why I can't make predictions about the future. And now perhaps you understand.'

His eyes searched hers and she nodded mutely and caught her breath when he told her rawly, 'I need you, but then you know that. When you left Italy I told myself it was for the best. You deserve so much more than I can offer. You're a warm, loving, generous woman; there's not a mean-spirited bone in your exquisite body. You should have everything—love, loyalty, marriage, kids—the whole package. I have no damned right to deny that to you—yet here I am, doing just that.'

He held her eyes with a slow-burning look, his sensual mouth soft. 'Hold me, *cara*. Whatever you decide about the future, I need to feel you against me now.'

Her senses reeling, she wrapped her arms around him, burrowing her head into his shoulder, boneless and helpless as one of his hands gently stroked her hair, the other splayed out against her ribcage, tantalisingly close to her breasts, and her breathing was shallow and ragged as he murmured, 'I want you here, with me, *carissima*—in my life, my home, my bed. I know you want it too.'

His hand slid upwards to curl softly round her breast and she closed her eyes, sucking in her breath as her flesh responded invitingly. She could feel the tension in him, the tiny tremors that told her his control was precarious, but leashed for the moment.

How could she deny him? How could she deny herself? He was all she ever wanted, and if her love was strong enough, vital enough, then surely it would breed love in him? But...

'I'm afraid,' she whispered truthfully, her hands clinging to him. Afraid of never being able to reach his heart, of the time when he would discover she'd become a habit rather than a challenge.

Habits got boring and he'd need to move on, working his way through a string of live-in women towards the time when he'd need to call it a day, settle down with some sophisticated female who wouldn't blink an eyelash at the type of loveless marriage he would offer, settle down to get his heirs.

Her heart would break when he asked her to leave.

'Don't be afraid,' he murmured softly against her ear, his tongue lapping her lobe. He was using unfair tactics, she decided muzzily, and discovered she didn't mind at all. She turned her mouth to his and he obliged, dropping tiny, tasting kisses as he whispered, 'It would be beautiful; everything would be beautiful, I promise. And I'd do nothing to stand in the way of your career—you've only recently discovered you're capable of carving one out for yourself. And that's important.'

His lips left hers and trailed down to her throat and she wriggled closer, as close as she could get, making a tiny, mewing, ecstatic sound. And he told her, satisfaction at her responses making his voice rich and dark, 'There would be times when we'd be separated. Work—yours or mine—could take us away for a while. I know I'd hate that, but we'd always know we were coming home to each other.'

Always! He'd said always! Unknowingly, maybe, but what did that matter? There was hope. There was!

Using that word, that wonderful word, in connection with their future relationship revealed more to her than he knew himself!

His lips were at the base of her throat now, his hands parting her white jacket. With the instinct of Eve, she wriggled voluptuously in his lap and heard the quickening of his heartbeats, the rasp of a shallow indrawn breath as her pouting breasts were revealed in their sinfully mere coverings of delicate white lace.

'*Carissima*—' His throat jerked, his eyes closing as if he was in pain. His hands tightened around her waist as he pushed her upright, away from him. Then he gently folded her jacket together, hiding her body. 'It would be too easy to take you, force you to admit that we belong together as lovers. Your body already knows that,' he told her thickly, a rough shake in his voice, 'but your mind must know it too, and want it, accept it. I won't touch you again, I promise, until you've decided to come to me.'

'I've already made my decision,' she whispered huskily, placing her tender hands on either side of his beloved face, loving the feel of the hard bones, the austerely beautiful features.

'And?' He went very still, his eyes piercing hers with sharp urgency. 'What have you decided, *cara*?'

She dropped her head, her eyes drowsy with love. 'That I will live with you, be with you.' And she almost added 'always', but held it back because the time was not yet right. But it would be. One day the time would be right. She had to believe that.

For a tiny moment she thought he hadn't heard her, but then his eyes darkened with passion, a wicked smile beginning to curl his lips as he growled, 'Well, in that case...' He reached behind him and, as if by magic, the lounger reclined. 'I'm too impatient for you to carry you to the bed we will share in the future. We will make love together in the sun.' Deftly, he slid her jacket away, his hands quickly dropping to the waistband of her skirt. 'No one can overlook us. There is no one to interrupt.'

With just a little help from her, he wriggled her skirt down over her hips, but removing her stockings was his undoing.

With a groan, he buried his head against her tiny lacy briefs, spasms of urgency shaking his strong body.

'Help me, Bess—help me. God! I need you so desperately!'

Tenderly, lingeringly, loving him more with each passion-filled moment, loving him more for his masculine vulnerability, she helped him all she could. She unbuttoned his shirt and slipped it from his powerful shoulders, running her fingers across the width of his chest before trailing them slowly down, tucking them beneath the waistband of his trousers, moving in tantalising exploration until he snatched them away, carrying the culprits to his mouth, kissing them fiercely.

And his voice was heavy as he exclaimed, 'Witch!' and turned the torment on her, stripping away her remaining garments until she was unashamedly naked, the sun caressing her supple body. Then he caught her in his strong arms, pulling her down, covering her body with his mouth, feverishly devouring her until she cried out for mercy, writhing with frenzied desire beneath him.

It was dusk when they finally smiled hazily into each other's eyes and Luca pushed her tumbled hair away from her face.

'You are beautiful. I can't have enough of you. Do you know that? But we have to get dressed,' he added regretfully. Then he smiled his slow, beautiful smile. 'We will help each other.' A lean finger trailed down between her breasts. 'It will take longer— much longer—but it will be far more exciting. And then, *carissima*, we will go together and fetch your things. Tell your friend she will have to find someone else to share with.'

Bess sat up slowly, wrapping her arms around her body, her eyes solemn. 'No, Luca. I can't.'

She saw his mouth tighten. 'You've changed your mind!' he accused harshly, and Bess shivered convulsively, feeling shy and awkward for the first time with him as he jerked upright, his hands grasping her upper arms, his fingers biting savagely into her flesh. 'You can't do that to me. You can't do that to us! I won't let you!'

'No,' she denied breathlessly. Her shimmering green eyes pleaded with him to understand. 'I haven't changed my mind. But it's the timing. After the weekend, I'll move in with you, I promise.' Her voice quivered. She was clinging onto her principles here; she did have a few of them left. And she was nervous; she couldn't help that. Living openly with her lover was a big step for a woman of hitherto impeccable principles to take.

But there was another principle involved too, she comforted herself. The principle of being true to the man you loved. And she did love Luca. More than life.

There was ice in his eyes now and she hated it. It shrivelled her. She began to scramble hurriedly into her clothes. He thought she was suffering an attack of the jitters and he didn't like it. But when she explained, properly, he would have to understand.

'Procrastinating, Bess?' he asked coldly, dragging on his shirt. 'Why put off what we both know is inevitable?'

'I am not!' she countered, tucking her stockings into her bag and pushing her bare feet into her shoes. 'But I can't move in with you until I've seen Tom and told him I can't marry him. It would be awful for him if he heard about us before I'd seen him. Try to understand.'

He stood up, towering over her, looking lean and dangerous. His eyes slid to her naked ring finger. 'You've had plenty of time to tell him. So why haven't you?' His eyes lifted to hers, full of dark suspicion. 'Hedging your bets, is that it? He'll marry you, I won't. Is that the problem? Is that why you haven't been able to bring yourself to tell him? Do you need time to work out which one of us would make the better bargain?

'Answer me, Bess,' he commanded, his voice rough-edged. 'Do a wedding ring and a piece of paper mean so much? Mean more to you than what we have? Such trappings can be totally meaningless, as I learned to my cost.'

'It's nothing like that,' she whispered miserably, hanging her head. The weight of his suspicious attack was bowing her down. 'I don't want to fight you over this, so please try to understand. I have to tell him face to face, not over the phone.'

'Right!' he said grimly. He glanced frowningly at his watch. 'I'll drive you down now. You can see him—tell him—tonight. We should be back here well before midnight.'

He was already stalking back into the house, collecting the jacket and tie he'd discarded much earlier, and Bess pattered after him, appalled.

She loved him to pieces—so much more, she was sure, than he would ever be able to love her—but he wasn't going to take charge of her life. People had been doing that from the day of her birth. She was determined to make her own decisions now.

'No, Luca.' She faced him, her small hands planted on her slender hips. 'I'll drive myself down on Sunday morning. I'll handle this my way or not at all,' she warned, hating to fight with him but knowing she must.

And she flinched, her face paling, as he asked coldly, 'Is that an ultimatum, Bess? Or blackmail? I don't accept either.'

'It's simply a fact.' She wasn't going to meekly back down now, no matter how much he meant to her. The issue was too important. It would set the tone for their future relationship. That was, if he still wanted one. The way he was looking at her now suggested it was the last thing on his mind.

She was taking a huge risk, she knew, but despite her inner turmoil her voice was calm as she told him, 'I've made up my mind. It doesn't only affect the two of us, Luca. There are other people to consider. Because after I've seen Tom I'll have to break the news to my parents. Tom's father is Dad's partner, after all. The two families are close. And it's too late tonight to do both. Surely you can see that? I need to try to minimise any bad feeling.'

Green eyes met the cold ice of his and something died inside her when he nodded abruptly, his face grim, his voice painfully polite, very cold as he said, 'As you wish. If you're ready I'll drive you home.'

# CHAPTER ELEVEN

LUCA was still sulking, Bess thought wretchedly as she took the lane out of Braylington that would eventually bring her to the Old Rectory. At least she devoutly hoped that his silence was nothing more than a fit of male pique. She'd heard nothing from him since she'd refused to let him drive her down here the other evening.

Once or twice on the silent journey back to the flat she'd been tempted to capitulate, to tell him, Go ahead, then; have it your way. I'll see Tom this evening if that's what it takes to get you talking to me again. But something had held her back and she was sure she'd done the right thing.

Instead she'd again tried to make him see it her way, telling him, 'If I moved in with you before I'd spoken to Tom face to face, my parents would be appalled. Particularly Mum. As it is she'll call it living in sin, go all dramatic about it and tell me I'm a fallen woman—all that sort of stuff.'

She'd tried to keep it light but he hadn't responded in the way she'd hoped, simply stating coldly, 'And you couldn't live with that. Despite everything, their good opinion is the only thing that matters.'

'That's not exactly fair, is it?' she'd replied heatedly, wishing the journey were over yet contrarily wishing it would last for ages, giving her time

to talk him round. She couldn't bear to say good-
night before this argument was resolved.

'Life's not fair,' he'd clipped back.

She'd gritted her teeth, counted to ten, then
denied, more or less calmly, 'You're wrong; their
opinion isn't the most important thing. But it does
matter to me. Why lose it if I don't have to? I've
always been what you could call a model daughter—
tried to please, kept myself in the background, never
done anything unexpected or caused them a moment's anxiety.' She'd flicked him a sideways look
but his face was still grim, set that way, she'd
guessed, because he simply wasn't used to not
having his own way.

She was, she'd decided, on a hiding to nothing
here, but had plodded on. 'They're both fond of
Tom and saw our engagement as ideally sensible.
When they learn I've given him his ring back and
intend moving in with you, they'll—'

'Leave it, will you?' He'd cut her short, his hands
gripping the steering wheel as if he'd have liked to
rip it from its moorings. 'I understand perfectly.
OK? So let's forget it, shall we?'

He really hadn't wanted to hear any more, she
thought now, had been unwilling to listen to how
she intended to do everything properly—break the
news to Tom first and then to her parents, letting
it sink in before explaining that she'd fallen in love
with Luca and would be moving in with him.

She wasn't looking forward to it.

In fact she was feeling physically sick as the car
tyres crunched to a gentle halt on the gravel drive.
The house looked peaceful in the warm morning
sunshine but she was about to break that serenity.

She cut the engine and sat for a moment listening to the silence, wondering if Luca would ever forgive her for refusing to give into his demands, wondering if she would be moving in with him after all, or whether he would tell her to forget it.

Her parents didn't know to expect her. She had telephoned twice, both times getting no answer, and had given up trying. They would be shocked by what they would regard as her bad behaviour, so turning up unexpectedly wouldn't be a big drama.

With a surge of sudden anguish she wished that Luca were there. She needed his support in this. The wanting made her feel ravaged. He'd offered his support, of course, under his own terms, but she'd refused it and must take the punishment.

She sighed heavily. She had to do this on her own.

Just then Helen walked out of the open front door and Bess watched her for a moment through the windscreen.

Wearing a creamy cotton sundress, her golden hair hanging loose down her back, she looked as wonderful as ever, the simple full-skirted style of the dress and the artless hairstyle making her look softer.

How would she feel when she learned that she and Luca were living together? Helen and Luca had recently—and, she suspected, briefly—been lovers. It wasn't something Bess liked thinking of, but she had to be adult about this.

Would Helen feel personally rejected? Bess truly hoped not. Or would she simply shrug it off as one of those things because, in her world, the rich and the famous were not known for their staying power when it came to love affairs?

Bess shivered bleakly. Would the strength of her love be enough to keep Luca with her? Or had he already written her off?

Her courage almost deserted her but she knew that whatever happened between her and Luca Vaccari she couldn't marry Tom. Besides, Helen had recognised her car by now and was slowly, reluctantly almost, walking in her direction.

She got out of the car and stared into her sister's face. Helen had never taken much notice of her so she was prepared for one of her usual dismissive looks. But the expression on those lovely features revealed something that looked remarkably like alarm, and her breathless, 'We didn't expect you this weekend,' did little to explain it away.

'I know Mum likes to be informed of visits—even from one of her own daughters—and preferably in writing,' Bess said drily. 'It was an impulse.' She couldn't explain why she was really here. Tom would hate to think that his arch-enemy had known about her decision before he had.

Helen shot her a wary, puzzled glance.

'You look different.' Her eyes raked over the slimly cut white jeans and loose cinnamon-coloured silk top Bess had chosen to wear for the drive down. 'I expect it's because your hair's not scraped back. At least you're not still wearing scarlet. You shouldn't, not with your colouring.'

She shrugged, as if the subject bored her. 'Listen, you've wasted your journey. Dad's playing golf and Ma's at the garden centre with Barbara Clayton. They'll probably go somewhere for lunch. And I'm tied up. I was on my way to the study when I thought I heard a car.' She swung round to face the house again, as if she couldn't wait to get away. 'I suppose Ma told you all about my business venture? It was supposed to be kept a secret until it was ready to go, but she can't keep her mouth shut for five minutes.'

It was Luca who'd explained about the wedding boutique but Bess wasn't going to go into that right now. Her mother's integrity would have to be re-inforced later, after she'd got the worst part of the day over. So she explained firmly, 'It's Tom I've really come to see,' and watched Helen's slim shoulders go rigid.

'Docs he know?' She sounded as if someone was trying to strangle her.

'No. I'll drive over to the Clayton place when I've snatched a coffee.'

'I— No, don't.' Helen's face was strangely flushed. 'What I mean is, I think he's working. I know he's got a lot on right now, so he's probably at the office. If you like I'll phone through and find out, save you a wasted trip. Why don't we—?' But whatever she'd been about to suggest was lost as the throaty roar of an engine slashed through the sunny rural silence.

Luca! Bess's heart made a series of crazy somer-saults as she watched him leave the vehicle he'd parked rakishly next to her own modest runabout. But then it slowed down to a dull, heavy beat as Helen floated towards him, her arms outstretched.

'Luke—darling! How lovely to see you! Oh!' She put her hands on his shoulders and reached up to plant a lingering kiss on his mouth. A very re-ceptive mouth, Bess noted with sinking dismay as

Luca's arms went around the gorgeous body and Helen tipped her head to gaze into his lazily smiling eyes. 'But you've been so naughty!' the ex-model chided. 'I've been expecting to hear from you every day since we parted in Italy. I've got something terribly important to discuss with you. But that can't come as a surprise, can it?'

Bess felt ill with jealousy. Helen obviously still thought of him as her property. They'd been lovers not so long ago. Her stomach kicked with pain. With the lovely ex-model so obviously still keen, would Luca choose to return to her?

Helen knew the score; she wouldn't bother him with principles. There was, Bess thought sickly, no competition. Helen was cooing, 'I tried phoning you a thousand times but was told you were incommunicado—even to me! What have you béen up to?'

He chose not to answer that. 'Making love to your little sister' wouldn't have gone down too well, Bess supposed. His head lifted and he stared at Bess over the gold of Helen's hair. The silvery eyes were cold and hard and she knew he was still bitterly angry with her for refusing to do exactly as she was told.

A look that told her it was all over between them? Was that it? Or was he still simply punishing her?

She must have made a sound of distress because Helen turned abruptly, her face pale now, her voice brittle as she said too brightly, 'She's on her way to see Tom. But we think he's working. I'll phone through for her. He might be at home. We don't want her to have a wasted journey back into town. Stay and talk to her, darling. When she goes we'll get together. I've got so much to talk to you about. Important stuff.'

She was off, almost at a run, in a flurry of creamy cotton skirts, and Bess thought dully that she needn't have gone to the trouble—very uncharacteristic in any case—because the way things looked she could spend the rest of the day tracking Tom down. She wouldn't have anything else to do.

He made no move to come to her. Slowly, Bess made her way over the gravel to him.

'Why are you here?' she asked unsteadily. After the silence of the last few days, considering the way he was looking at her now, with no pleasure at all, and vividly recalling the fond expression on his face when Helen had hurled herself at him, it was stupid to hope he'd come along to lend his support when she told her parents she'd ended her engagement to Tom.

Even so, the flicker of hope refused to die, so when he informed her coldly, 'To protect my investment, what else?' she could have died of the pain he inflicted.

His company had given Helen's business idea the financial backing needed to get it off the ground, of course. But did bankers normally make unexpected visits to very minor clients on lazy Sunday mornings? She didn't think so.

There had to be a whole lot more behind his visit than that. Helen, it was obvious, would be only too happy to resume their past intimate relationship.

Sick with misery, she turned as her sister came out of the house.

'I checked for you. He is working. So off you go! You needn't hang around here for that coffee.

Tom will give you some.' She was acting as if she couldn't wait to get rid of her. Her eyes were feverishly bright and she seemed wound up to the point of explosion—due, Bess decided, to the way her former lover had turned up, under the pretext of a business meeting...

Mutely, Bess turned to Luca, but he said nothing, his eyes dark, enigmatic, boring remorselessly into hers—as if he couldn't wait to see the back of her either and was willing her to go. And before he could see the sudden anguished tears in her eyes she went to her car and started the engine, driving away from Luca's cold eyes, Helen's vibrant loveliness, away from the swirling undercurrents, the atmosphere that was alive with terrible tension.

But maybe she was being paranoid, Bess thought edgily as she drove back into the sleepy Sunday morning market town. Luca wasn't the type of man to play one sister off against the other, pick a woman up and drop her because she refused to do what he wanted her to do? Was he?

No, she could never have fallen so deeply in love with that type of man; surely some sixth sense would have warned her, told her he wasn't to be trusted.

And yet, seeing him this morning, she hadn't found a trace of the man she loved. The lover, the dear companion, seemed to have vanished, leaving just a hard-edged stranger.

Realising she'd driven past the Clayton and Ryland offices, she gave an exasperated growl at her own wool-gathering and reversed with more speed than neatness into a parking space, only to find Tom's sedate saloon pulling in beside her.

He looked red in the face, she noted as she locked her car door. As if he'd been doing something in an almighty hurry, or was deeply embarrassed—which couldn't be the case. And the sight of him fumbling with the controls, getting out of the vehicle so awkwardly, his movements jerky, did something to ease her own nervousness temporarily out of the way.

Overwork, she decided sympathetically.

'Helen told me you were already hard at it in the office.'

'Yes. Well. I had to dash out for—something.' He fidgeted with the collar of his shirt. 'Did she say anything else?'

About what? she wondered. Helen had told her everyone was out, tied up, too busy to spend time with her, implying that she might as well go back to where she had come from. Nothing else. She shook her head.

'Then you'd better come in,' he said heavily, fishing the doorkeys from his pocket. And she followed him, having to force herself because the trepidation was back again in barrow-loads.

She was going to hurt him and she hated the thought. True, he wasn't passionately in love with her, just as, so she had discovered, she wasn't in love with him. But he saw her as a suitable life partner and he didn't like his carefully laid plans altered by so much as an inch. She heaved a great sigh.

Hearing it, he looked at her worriedly. 'Take a pew and mind how you go.'

A necessary warning because, as always the floor space was covered with piles of dry-looking, dog-eared legal documents. She picked her way through them carefully, and when she got herself seated he was already standing on the other side of the enormous desk.

He looked as if he was at a funeral, she decided, and put the miserable, hangdog expression down to his hating to be interrupted while he was trying to work. She would say what she had to say and leave.

Her fingers stiff and lifeless, she dug in her handbag and produced his ring. Placing it carefully on his desk, she said quietly, 'Tom—I can't marry you. I'm sorry about this, truly.' She paused awkwardly, waiting for an explosion from him, and when it didn't come said quickly, 'We've always been friends, you and I, and that friendship's always meant a lot to me. We both thought marriage was the next natural step, but we were wrong.

'Tom, I didn't reach this decision lightly, and I'm sure you'll agree with me when you've had time to think about it.' Her eyes met his pleadingly, willing him to understand, as she added softly, 'I'll always think of you with affection, but that's not enough, is it?'

'No, I suppose not,' he answered quickly, not meeting her eyes. But he raised his head, as if forcing himself to look at her. 'I do understand,' he said gruffly, then seemed about to say something else but obviously changed his mind, and his shoulders, which had been up round his ears, suddenly relaxed. He looked, she thought bemusedly, like a man who'd just had a weight taken from his mind.

Which wasn't as crazy as it seemed, she told herself as she drove back to the Old Rectory. He hadn't stormed and blustered, heaped recriminations on her head, because he was a decent sort. And he too could have been having grave doubts about their future together, perhaps wondering if their tame relationship and her unexpected outbreak of independence were things he could live with.

But Tom, being thoroughly honourable, wouldn't have been the one to make the first move.

So it was over, she realised at last, and without the scenes she had so dreaded. All she had to do now was convince her parents the break was for the best, and get on with the rest of her life.

But would the rest of her life include Luca?

She couldn't bear to think it wouldn't. She couldn't bear it and so she wouldn't think it! Besides, despite his silence over the last few days, the unfeeling way he'd looked at her this morning, he couldn't have cut her out of his life. He couldn't. She wouldn't let herself believe it.

He'd been so open, so honest. He had never promised something he couldn't deliver.

And if he'd been annoyed with her, well, it was only to be expected, wasn't it? He was unused to the experience of not getting everything he wanted, when he wanted it.

Now that she'd talked herself into a more positive frame of mind, her heart was considerably lighter when she hurried into the house.

Luca's car was still there on the drive, and she would soon be able to tell him she was now free, her own woman, happy to move in with him, dedicate her future to making him fall in love with her, truly in love, making their relationship permanent, lasting as long as they both should live. The love affair of a lifetime she so desperately craved.

Only she wouldn't tell him that last bit, of course, just work on it!

The house was silent, filled with the scent of the early summer flowers her mother picked from the garden. She went straight through to the sitting room, looking for Luca, and found him pacing the floor.

He turned sharply as she entered, his features tight and austere. He seemed, she thought, her breath catching in her throat, as if he was under enormous pressure, savagely reining back dark emotions.

Her bright confidence drained right out of her, the words she'd planned dying away. He looked so forbidding, so far away. Already lost to her? She wouldn't know unless she asked.

'Where's Helen?' she asked inanely. She didn't want to know where her sister was and could have kicked herself for her wimpy cowardice.

'Making coffee.' His voice was flat; he sounded almost exhausted. Bess bit down on her lower lip. What was wrong here? Wasn't he at all interested to know how her meeting with Tom had gone? Why had he changed so dramatically?

She wanted to melt into the wallpaper, hide herself away, but she remembered the sheer exuberance with which Helen had flung herself into his arms and decided firmly that she was never going to melt into the background again.

What Helen could do, she could do!

Bravely, she took the necessary paces to close the distance between them, lifting her face to his as she wound her arms around his neck, pulling his head down.

For a few hateful, hope-killing moments his lips were icy beneath hers, but she shuddered with a relief that was almost uncontainable as she heard him give a deep, unsteady breath before his arms came around her, pulling her body into his, kissing her deeply, almost desperately, as if this were the last he would have of her.

Everything was all right! He couldn't kiss her with such devouring urgency if he didn't still want her, she thought dizzily, clinging to him, only surfacing from the ecstatic turbulence as the rattle of china warned her of Helen's presence.

And Luca heard it too, must have done, because his body went very still, his head lifting, his arms dropping away from her in slow motion.

'Luke, darling—Daddy's just got home.' Her voice was hectically bright, even by Helen's standards. 'He's gone through to the study to pour drinks. Could you go, darling?' She put the tray of coffee things down on a side table, and pushed a swathe of golden hair back from her flushed face. 'You can explain that clause in the contract to him. I can't make head nor tail of it!'

She sounded as if she couldn't wait for him to go, and after a tight, impatient nod of his dark head Luca stalked out of the room, and Bess knew—she just knew—that her sister couldn't have failed to witness that passionate embrace because her face was ashy-pale now as she slowly turned on her heels to face her.

'You saw Tom? Spoke to him?' Her voice was low, breathlessly awkward. 'Are you all right?'

So she'd guessed what had been happening, Bess thought sombrely. After walking in, witnessing that kiss, she'd rapidly put two and two together, realising that she and Luca were far more than comparative strangers. At least it made her explanation easier.

'I gave him his ring back,' she answered edgily. 'But then you already know that, don't you?'

'I—' Helen's face went scarlet. She turned quickly, her back to Bess as she poured coffee. And her voice was oddly muffled as she commiserated, 'Darling—I honestly don't know what to say. Look, if it's any consolation, you'll find someone else. The way you're looking these days you won't find it a problem.'

She turned with an offering of coffee but her hand was shaking so badly that she put it hurriedly back on the tray. And Bess stared at her, confused.

No one, walking in just now, could have mistaken that embrace for anything other than what it was: a passionate, savagely hungry kiss between two lovers. So Helen had to know that she'd already found someone else.

And it was Tom she should be sympathising with, wasn't it? Someone, somewhere, had got their wires crossed. But then Helen had never liked Tom. Sometimes Bess had thought they violently hated each other. So her sister was probably delighted that she wouldn't have to put up with him as her brother-in-law.

As her thoughts whirled round and round inside her head she got more confused by the second, and Helen's anxious face didn't help any. But when the other woman said earnestly, 'My pregnancy wasn't planned, darling, I promise you. I didn't do it deliberately to take him away from you,' everything became horribly clear.

Bess felt for the arm of the chair she was standing near and sank down heavily, all the strength in her legs draining away. She stared blankly at her sister's anxious face, unable to avoid the killing truth.

Because of what she'd seen, Helen had guessed that she'd come here today to break off her engagement; that Luca was very definitely in the picture. 'You'll find someone else,' she'd promised. Warned? She might just as well have said, You don't want stodgy old Tom and I can't blame you. But you can't have Luke. He's mine. I'm carrying his child.

Amazingly, Helen looked more placid now, kneeling in front of her, taking her icy hands in her own. Her voice was soft as she murmured, 'He always wanted children at some stage—to carry on the family business. Well, you must have been aware of that, discussed it. Knowing him, it would have been one of the first things he warned you of.'

Oh, sure they'd discussed it, Bess thought on a wave of sickening bitterness. Sure he'd warned her that if and when he remarried it would be to get an heir to carry on after him in the complicated Vaccari financial empire. And Helen rammed it home as she increased the pressure of her hands.

'It just happened a damn sight sooner than he expected, that's all. We hadn't meant—

'Anyway...' she sucked in a breath, unable now to disguise her triumphant radiance '... if it means anything to you, which I don't suppose it does right now, I do love him, quite madly. I'll make him the perfect wife, I promise.'

As if that made everything all right, Bess thought wretchedly. As if that would take away the pain that was like a rusty knife hacking cruelly at her heart.

She withdrew her hands from Helen's, wrapping her arms around her shaking body.

It was all hatefully clear. Luca had had an affair with Helen. That was fact. He hadn't intended to get her pregnant. That was unfortunate.

But he'd had to go through the bitter experience of knowing that a child of his had been aborted. He wouldn't allow that to happen again.

Had Helen written to him, telling him the news? She'd stated that she hadn't been able to reach him by phone. Had he received the letter immediately after he'd asked her, Bess, to have an affair with him? It seemed to make sense. It would account for his deep silence over the past few days, the way he'd distanced himself from her, Helen's ecstatic welcome.

They'd had time to discuss future plans, wedding plans, while she'd been with Tom. Luca had told her he'd had no intention of marrying Helen, and the clearing up of the misunderstanding had opened the way for her to be with him. But he was going to have to marry Helen now.

And hadn't she seen the emotional pressure he'd been under when she'd walked in and found him pacing the room?

The way he'd responded when she'd virtually forced him to kiss her had told her he still wanted her sexually. But Helen was carrying his child and he wouldn't desert her.

Willing some strength back into her body, she got shakily to her feet and walked blindly to the door, and Helen blurted out anxiously, 'Where are you going?'

She wanted to say, Don't worry, I'm not going to find him and make a terrible scene. But she couldn't rake up the energy.

'Home,' she answered drainingly.

'Oh—I don't think—' Helen was twisting her hands together. This was the first time, Bess thought wryly, that her sister had ever shown any concern for her well-being. 'I know it's come as a terrible shock. But you and Luke—'

'No!' Bess cut her off savagely. She was not going to discuss her relationship with Luca. Hadn't Helen, as always, got her own way? Jumped right in and taken just what she wanted?

Walking quickly out of the house, she realised that she absolutely must stop thinking of him as Luca.

On a wave of triumph that was completely hollow and desperately short-lived, she reflected that he'd obviously never asked Helen to use his birth name.

But that signified absolutely nothing at all. Not in the end.

# CHAPTER TWELVE

IT WAS late when Luke pushed his way past her into Niccy's apartment.

Thankful that her friend was out partying, according to the note that had been left propped on the kitchen table, Bess would nevertheless have given anything to avoid this final confrontation.

She would have thought that he'd have accepted her discreet departure from his life and been thankful. She hadn't bargained on seeing him again—certainly not so soon, anyway. She wouldn't be attending the wedding, and didn't think she'd be able to face the christening either.

Had he come to chew everything over? Had he really got that much nerve? Or had he come to apologise, perhaps, express his regret for the way things had turned out? Didn't he realise it would only make her feel a thousand times worse?

'Where the hell have you been?' he demanded harshly, his eyes raking over her. 'I've been phoning this place every half-hour since I got back. I eventually got your flatmate, who said she hadn't seen you. I gave up in the end and came round to camp on the doorstep if necessary.'

'Here and there,' she answered thinly, praying to heaven that he wouldn't try to touch her. It would finish her if he did—her control was desperately precarious.

She'd spent hours driving around, aimlessly, trying not to think, until she'd found a park to sit in, and had forced herself to face her future, make plans for her own preservation.

She wouldn't let him mess up her life again. And the way he was looking at her now, with rawly savage need, made her deeply, suspiciously wary.

'I was worried about you,' he said, explaining the flash of anger. 'When you simply disappeared I realised that you probably needed a little time on your own to come to terms with Helen's news. It will have come as a shock, but it doesn't change anything between us, of course. However, I did understand. But as the hours dragged by and I couldn't contact you I began to imagine the worst.' His mouth curved in a wry, self-mocking smile. 'I even contacted the police and the hospitals to find out if you'd been in a traffic accident.'

Had he really been that worried? Did he truly care about her? A shudder of weakness dragged through her and she lowered her eyes, not looking at him, armouring herself.

Was he really about to tell her that Helen's pregnancy had been a mistake? Well, they all knew that, didn't they? Was he really going to say that it was a mistake he couldn't ignore, that he could only put right by marrying her sister, giving his child his name and protection, but that he still wanted her, Bess?

Would he offer to set her up in an apartment of her own, visiting her discreetly when time allowed?

After all, as far as he was concerned, little had changed, just as he had stated. He had made it plain that he wouldn't marry her, envisaging his remarriage as a possibility for the future, the sole object being to secure an heir. The getting of an heir had happened sooner than he'd planned. But nothing else had changed.

The thought appalled her. She watched his eyes change to pools of deepest silver and her breath shuddered in her lungs. Dear God, how easily he had made her love him. She had been swamped by him, overwhelmed, dragged deep into the mystery of his male perfection, his careless domination of her senses.

'You told Tom you couldn't marry him?' His voice had gentled alarmingly. Bess knew she had to be very, very careful. He must never know how easily he could make her betray every last one of her principles, behave in a way that would make her deeply ashamed of herself for the rest of her life.

She dug for the same thin voice and employed it. 'Why ask? I'm sure you know I have.'

'*Cara*?' He lifted an eyebrow in query. Her attitude was confusing him and she could understand that—after the embrace she had practically forced on him earlier.

She had to make him go away before she lost all her self-respect and agreed to anything and everything he wanted.

And telling him that she refused to be her brother-in-law's mistress wouldn't cut any ice. It would only make him work harder to prove that she could, that his marriage would be one of expediency, that she, Bess, was the woman he really wanted.

Wanted for now, added a cynical voice inside her head. It helped. She ignored the hands he was holding out to her and gave him back a stony look.

'Can't you take a hint? Do I really have to spell it out?'

He sighed, his sensual mouth softening as he invited with all the temptation of the devil himself, 'You're so upset, so talk it through. I can understand how you feel. It can't have been easy, hearing the details of Helen's pregnancy. But we can talk it out, together. Together, we can do anything, *carissima*.'

She walked to the door, and how she ever got herself there she would never know. Her legs were jerky, her whole body rigid with outrage. What a louse! He was trying to tell her that Helen's baby was a blip they could conveniently ignore, something he could sweet-talk her into disregarding!

A terrible pain bit through her anger and she hoped to heaven that he wouldn't detect it in her voice. She snatched at the handle and flung the door wide.

'That's just the point,' she said coldly. 'There is no more "together".' Sweet Lord, she had to keep this up, to make him leave. Only then could she begin to nurse her wounds, try to pick up the pieces. 'It was great while it lasted, and just for a while I did think . . .' She allowed her words to tail away and managed to produce a throwaway shrug. 'But on consideration it's better if we don't see each other again.'

She battled with the agony, fought it down, desperately reminding herself of the escape plan she'd made. Any time now, either she or Mark was going to have to visit the States. There were promising venues in New England to see. She'd plead with Mark to let her go. She'd go down on her knees if she had to.

'Why?' he demanded harshly. He'd joined her at the pointedly open door. Fierce silver eyes stabbed her like a knife. 'You once told me you loved me. Remember?'

Bess closed her eyes on a swamping wave of grief. How could she ever forget? Please God, don't let me cry, she prayed fervently. Give me the strength . . .

'Isn't that what people always say in that kind of situation?' She swallowed on the terrible lie. 'Anyway, you said it was lust, and I have to hand it to you—you were right.' She heard the savage snarl of his breath and made herself ignore it. 'But that's not the point, not really, not now. What I'm doing my best to make you understand is that I want to get on with the rest of my life, on my own terms. You should understand that. After all, you were in some respects responsible for the metamorphosis.'

She couldn't look at him. She dared not. But she could feel the shock waves of his icy anger bombarding her like a hail of frozen meteors.

'Did I say you wouldn't have a life of your own?' he lashed. 'If I remember correctly, and I do, I stated precisely the opposite.'

She nodded wearily. But, determined to make one last effort, she rallied herself desperately, refusing to allow herself to weaken.

'I don't want to be your mistress,' she told him flatly. 'I won't jump from one pigeon-hole into another—from Tom's suitable fiancée to your mistress.'

She didn't see him walk away. She didn't hear him go. She only knew he was no longer near her by the awful emptiness, by the aching void he'd left behind, by the bleak and terrible feeling of loss ...

Bess unpacked the few essentials she'd carried in her hand luggage and decided they'd do. No need to go to the trouble of raiding the suitcases she'd left in the safekeeping of the hotel porter. Besides, she was too tired to phone down and ask for them to be sent up.

After a month in New England, where she'd eventually signed up a wonderful hotel complex a few miles up the coast from Rockport where their clients, besides being luxuriously pampered, could go out on whale-spotting expeditions or inland and deeper into the lovely countryside for the glorious autumn colours—and all within easy reach of fashionable Boston—it felt strange to be back in Europe.

Particularly in Rome.

But Rome wasn't Tuscany and Luke was well and truly married to Helen.

And that was in the past, she reminded herself, and the working trip to the States had helped concentrate her mind. She hadn't even had to beg to be allowed to go. Mark must have taken one look at her haunted face and decided to send her halfway across the world to rid the office of her depressing influence!

Her lips indented slightly as she eased her shoes off her aching feet. She was sure that no one had guessed the reason for her misery. Except Niccy. And when she'd been told what had happened she'd vowed, 'If he ever shows his face here, asking for you, I'll kill him with my bare hands—and tell him why afterwards!'

And Mark hadn't flickered an eyelash when, on the eve of her hurried departure, she'd asked him not to tell anyone—and that meant *anyone*—where she could be contacted.

She'd known that she looked like a burst balloon—she'd certainly felt like one, that day at the office—and he'd merely said, 'Boyfriend trouble? Well, so long as you're not wanted by MI5 my lips are sealed.'

Not that Luca—Luke—would think of trying to get in touch with her. She'd told him all sorts of untruths to make him leave her alone. He must have thought she was the ex-lover from hell and been glad to have her right out of his life.

But she hadn't wanted her mother phoning long-distance, or writing volumes, badgering her about her broken engagement to poor, dear Tom, rubbing salt in the terrible wound by gloating on about how well Helen had done for herself, catching the highly eligible Luke Vaccari—and hadn't she told everyone it was on the cards and wasn't a mother's instinct always right?—and urging her to do her best to get back in time for the wedding.

That she could do without!

It had been bad enough knowing exactly when the wedding was taking place. During one of her routine calls back to base, Mark had told her, 'I've had your mother on the phone again, asking for a contact number—even though I've repeatedly as-

sured the good lady that you're well, happy,
working hard, moving around and difficult to pin
down.

'Anyway, she left a message for me to pass on
when you phoned in next. Roughly edited out for
sheer length, it's to tell you that Helen's wedding
is set for the twentieth. This month. She, your
father and Helen would like for you to be there,
but will understand if you can't make it. OK?'

The twentieth had been just over a week ago.
Helen wouldn't have wanted to hang around until
she had a definite bump in her middle. Her wedding
gown—no doubt a sumptuous clingy thing—
wouldn't have hung properly! She would have
looked less than perfect!

Bess had allowed herself that slight balm of
bitchiness then thrown herself back into her work,
and then, just hours before she'd been due to fly
back to the UK, Mark had faxed through an urgent
message asking her to make a small detour, stopping
off in Rome.

She had never wanted to visit Italy again. Her
memories of her short time here hurt too much.
But Mark had been tied up, so Bess had had to try
her teeth on a little problem. And ever since she'd
landed—or almost—she'd been ironing things out.

The driver assigned to their clients—a middle-
aged couple and their teenage daughter, staying in
this hand-picked hotel—had done a bunk, taking
the car. Which hadn't pleased anyone.

By the time she'd contacted the *polizia* with the
help of the hotel manager, who'd acted as trans-
lator, and learned that the absconding driver had
already been picked up in Naples, and that the car

could be collected any time, she'd already hired
another driver, making sure his references were impeccable, and an even more luxurious car, soothed
the clients, assured them of Jenson's best attention
at all times, and narrowly avoided collapsing with
sheer exhaustion.

'Mission accomplished,' she'd told Mark over the
phone, utterly weary but pleased with the way she'd
handled things, accepting without argument when
he'd offered,

'Stay over for a couple of days or so. I've checked
with the manager and there's a single room
available. You've earned a short break—expenses
paid.'

Earned or not, she had no real objections to
taking a breather. And here was as good a place as
any. After all, there were hurtful memories waiting
for her back in England, too. Not to mention the
inevitable and inexhaustible run-down on the
wedding which would come from her mother, plus
the delight at the prospect of the coming first
grandchild, all laced with stringent grumbles about
her stupidity in turning Tom down for no good
reason that anyone could see.

So to hell with jet lag. She would see all she could
of Rome in the next day or so. Visit all the picture-
postcard sights. Make like a tourist. Tomorrow.
Right now she felt too tired to put one foot in front
of the other.

Straightening her weary shoulders, she walked
slowly across the luxurious room she'd been given
and stood by the tall window. The view was glorious. Perched on a hill, the hotel was set in its own

typically Italianate gardens, and suddenly her eyes filled with tears.

Why couldn't she get him out of her head? Even a view, shimmering beneath the heat of the Italian sun, brought him back—so close that she felt she only had to stretch out her hand to touch him.

No matter how hard she tried, she kept remembering things about him. Things she would rather forget, wipe out of her mind for ever.

His passion, his warmth, the ability he had to make her feel as if she was the only woman in the universe . . . the terrible pain in his voice when he'd talked of the child he had lost . . . the spell he'd cast over her, binding her, blinding her to everything but the need to be with him . . .

Scrubbing her eyes angrily, she turned from the window. She wouldn't cry. She would stop thinking of him. She would never think of him again.

And she wouldn't think of the stupidity of that affirmation, either—the fact that he was now her brother-in-law, that in a few months' time Helen would produce her nephew or niece, that unless she went to live and work on the other side of the world she wouldn't be able to avoid contact indefinitely.

It didn't bear thinking about. So she wouldn't.

A discreet tapping on the door made her frown, and she dragged her fingers over her face to remove any lingering traces of dampness.

'*Avanti*!' she called resignedly, expecting a chambermaid, surprised but pleased when Signor Velardi walked in. The hotel manager was short and round with shiny black hair and a very white smile. She liked him a lot. He'd been invaluable this

afternoon, helping her with her dealings with the
police.

'*Signorina*—I check you have everything you
need. You are happy with your room?'

'It's perfect.' Bess found a smile, hating the
concern in his dark eyes. Could he tell she'd been
crying? What must he think of Jenson's if their
representative dissolved into tears after sorting out
a minor inconvenience?

So when he said, his liquid eyes full of sympathy,
'After your problems today you will want to rest.
I will personally see that a tray of tea is brought
up to you,' Bess countered immediately, 'That's
thoughtful of you, but I'm going out. There's so
much to see and I won't be here long. I want to
take in as much as I can.' And she flashed him a
smile and tried to look bright.

Launching straight into a round of hectic sight-
seeing was a great idea. It would stop her
thinking . . .

'Such stamina!' the little man said admiringly.
'A long flight, a troubled few hours, and still so
eager! May I suggest the Borghese Gardens?' he
inserted smoothly. 'Not far, and very peaceful.'

He smiled himself out and Bess grabbed a pair
of jeans and a loose sleeveless T-shirt out of her
flight bag and stripped off the classic navy blue
summer suit she'd been wearing. Emerging from
the shower ten minutes later, she dressed hurriedly,
grabbed the complimentary guidebook, stuffed it
into her bag and practically ran from the room, her
tiredness ignored because anything was better than
hanging around, waiting for her body clock to
adjust to the new time zone, letting her head fill

with thoughts, memories she had no wish to dwell on.

The sumptuous first-floor corridors were decorated and furnished in white and soft tobacco shades, crystal chandeliers sparkled overhead and exquisite floral arrangements perfumed the air.

The professional part of her brain approved the atmosphere of luxury while another part insisted on reminding her that nowhere was special or exciting now that Luke could never be part of her life.

But she wasn't going to think about him, was she? Tightening her mouth, she ignored the lifts and took the sweeping marble staircase, intent on getting outside, finding something—anything—to occupy her wretchedly wayward mind.

Pausing at the foot of the stairs, she fished out her guidebook and buried her nose in it, oblivious to the scattering of elegant guests who were relaxing in armchairs, sipping ice-cold drinks or simply people-watching.

The Borghese Gardens were fairly close, she noted, and Signor Velardi's suggestion that she visit them was tempting. But perhaps her state of mind demanded somewhere more crowded, brimming with life...

Suddenly the book she was poring over so intently was unceremoniously plucked from her hands, warm, hard fingers gripping her elbow.

Startled, deeply affronted, Bess tipped up her head and glared. Then began shaking. She couldn't breathe.

Luke!

It couldn't be. But it was. Were he and Helen honeymooning here? In this very hotel? Fate couldn't be that cruel!

Could it?

# CHAPTER THIRTEEN

'LUKE!' Bess whispered, her face stricken. Her pulses were beating so fiercely, so erratically, she thought she was going to faint.

'Luca,' he reminded her grimly. His hand tightened around her arm. 'Come on, we're getting out of here.'

Helplessly, she gazed up at him. His mouth was crooked, his silver eyes glittering. He looked very determined, strong emotions tightly leashed but simmering fiercely under the surface.

'Outside,' he repeated with dangerous softness. 'Unless you want the sort of scene that would set the whole of Rome talking for a week.'

Scene or not, she hadn't the strength to resist. His nearness, the sheer unexpectedness of the encounter, had weakened her until she could barely stand upright.

Sure that everyone must be looking at them—the sexy, smouldering male casually dressed in elegantly cut, hip-hugging black trousers and a dazzlingly white silk shirt, and the very ordinary female in her run-of-the mill jeans, her make-up-less face blotchy from crying—Bess kept her head low, her mind going round in futile circles.

Were they really honeymooning here? A dreadful coincidence? Was he as appalled as he'd sounded to have practically bumped right into her? And where was Helen? Waiting for him in their hotel bedroom, eager for his return?

Or was she hallucinating? Conjuring him out of the ether because he was her lost love, the only person in the world she needed to be near?

'In,' he commanded tersley, opening the passenger door of the car parked at the foot of the impressive steps down which he'd hustled her. 'We're going somewhere quiet where we can talk.'

The car was a low, dark, snarly-looking thing. Even without the engine running it seemed to vibrate with power.

Bess looked at him warily. She had never seen him like this before. He had turned into an out-and-out bully and she only had to glance at his hard, lean features to know that he wouldn't take no for an answer, not even if she screamed it until her throat was raw.

Nevertheless, she found herself saying, 'We can talk right here. I don't think I want to hear it, whatever it is. But go ahead, if you must.'

She wasn't going anywhere with him. She couldn't trust herself. She felt bad enough about betraying Tom—even though at the time she had already decided she could never marry him. She would fight to the last breath in her body before she would allow herself to betray her sister.

And fight she would have to, she recognised sickly. He was looking at her as if he could willingly strangle her, so the danger didn't come from him. It came from within her, deep within her, from the terrible yearning to touch him, hold him, be part of him for one last time...

She gave a strangled gasp at her own incurable weakness and he put her in the passenger seat with inescapable firmness and strapped her in. And her giddy head was still swimming as he joined her in the state-of-the-art vehicle, fired the ignition and smoothly pulled away.

She had to get a grip on herself, she knew that, and managed to croak, 'Where do you think you're taking me? And where's Helen? If you're planning a sisters' reunion party, forget it. She won't want me around on her honeymoon.'

'Too right, she won't. At a guess, you're the last person she'd want to see. You'd only make them both feel guilty and spoil their fun.'

Puzzled, Bess shot a look at him from beneath her lashes. He was smiling, damn him! Was he actually laughing at her? Had she said something amusing—or what?

'I don't know what you're talking about,' she muttered darkly, reminded that when they'd first met he'd talked in riddles, making her feel a fool because she hadn't understood what he was getting at.

He said gently, 'Shut up, do. I'm trying to concentrate. If we start talking things out now you'll claim my exclusive attention and we'll both land up in hospital.'

He had a point, she thought on a draining sigh. The traffic conditions were scary, everyone driving far too fast, diving for their slice of the road with typical Italian machismo.

But his hands were relaxed on the wheel; he obviously knew what he was doing, where he was going, and the small smile played around the

corners of his gorgeous mouth and somehow that
relaxed her too. Although it shouldn't have.

She sagged back against the soft leather up-
holstery. Her head was beginning to ache. It was
very warm, and she was desperately tired; the strain
of meeting up with him on top of everything else
was poleaxing her.

And even though she did her best to stay alert,
ready to shoot him down in flames if he so much
as mentioned the word mistress, her eyelids felt
heavier and heavier and she finally gave up the
hopeless attempt to keep them open and drifted off
to sleep.

She woke with a jolt. It was dusk. The car had
stopped. She was alone.

Blinking, she peered through the windscreen. She
could make out the heavy, dark shapes of trees, the
hazy outline of mountains against the deepening
sky. Somewhere a small animal squeaked in the
night and she shivered. Where was Luca?

Her heart began to flutter frantically, her nerves
all on edge. When the door at her side opened she
gave a startled yelp and he leaned in, telling her
lightly, 'Out you get, sleepyhead.'

'Where to?' she asked tightly, with deep suspicion. She wasn't going to let him know how re-
lieved she was to see him. Besides, it had taken him
a hell of a long time to find a quiet place to talk!
From the dusk-restricted view they appeared to be
at the end of nowhere.

'Our overnight accommodation.'

Oh, hell! Bess agonised, tears of sheer fright
flooding her eyes. He did want them to take up
where they'd left off—why else would he have

brought her here, miles from anywhere? And where had he put Helen? In a box labelled 'Take Out Only When Needed'?

He'd been married less than two weeks and his wife was expecting their child. The brush-off she'd given him obviously hadn't been nearly stringent enough. What would it take to make him give her up as a lost cause? And did he really want her so much that he would go to these lengths? To her shame, the thought excited as much as terrified her.

'Take me back to Rome,' she commanded, anchoring herself to her seat, folding her arms across her chest and looking, she devoutly hoped, as if nothing short of an earthquake would move her.

The car door opened wider and strong arms hauled her out. And fear of the hot surge of desire that coursed through her gave her the protection of anger, enabling her to produce a blistering, 'Let go of me, you rat!' and giving her the energy to thrash her limbs wildly, beat his silk-clad chest with her fists. 'You made me betray my principles before— I'll kill you before you make me do it again!'

'You mean Tom,' he said lightly, dismissively. Sublimely ignoring her frantic efforts to get free, he carried her effortlessly towards what looked like an old farmhouse. 'You didn't betray him. You knew what you were doing. The only person you ever betrayed was yourself, when you stupidly agreed to marry him.'

He shouldered open a heavy wooden door. It scraped on flagstones. Bess hissed, 'That's as maybe! But you're married to Helen now and I never wanted to have to see you again. Ever!' Her words throbbed with the intensity of her emotions and in the soft light of a lamp set on the central table she saw him grin, which made her redouble her efforts to beat him to a pulp. 'Put me down!'

He merely held her closer to his warm, hard body, putting his mouth close to her ear as he whispered wickedly, 'For a woman in love, you're playing very hard to get.'

'I...' Words failed her. Oh, what a loathsome rat! He clearly hadn't believed her when she'd told him she'd only said she loved him because that was what people said when they had sex together and wanted to dress it up, pretend it wasn't plain old-fashioned lust.

He was going to play on that, squeeze her poor battered heart until it bled, take cruel advantage of her devotion, use her precariously controlled emotions for his own sinful ends. She couldn't possibly be in love with a man like that!

'Evil swine!' she hissed, the animal ferocity of the abuse negated by the weak tears that flooded her eyes, the pain that clutched her heart making her whimper.

'Hush,' he said softly, brushing the tears away with his fingers. 'Sit quietly and try to relax a little while I make a fire.' He put her down on a peculiar sofa which felt as if it was stuffed with brick-ends and sharp sticks. So how the hell was she supposed to relax?

She shivered with tension, wrapping her arms around her body. It was cold in this stone room. They must be high in the mountains.

'If you've brought me here to persuade me to be your mistress,' she grated at his broad back as he hunkered down to put a match to the kindling in the huge recessed hearth, 'then you need educating. Don't you know you're supposed to provide soft lights, roses, gallons of champagne and a luxurious bed? Not a hovel and an implement of torture designed to loosely resemble something to sit on!'

She shot to her feet, her face scarlet with a mixture of anger and misery spiced with a blistering disappointment in her own judgement. How could she have fallen in love with such a creature? 'I want to go back to Rome. Now. And if you won't take me I'll walk.'

He said nothing. Just stood upright, brushing his hands off, smiling at her. The kindling flared, making the shadows dance, carving out his beautiful features with light and shade. Her throat thickened impossibly, and the pain and anger grew inside her.

She shot at him nastily, 'What is this dump?'

'Our trysting place?' he offered with a grin. 'Love-nest?'

'I'd rather be made love to in a bus shelter!' she blistered, and saw him lift his wide shoulders in an eloquent Latin shrug.

'It belongs to Alessandro, one of my many cousins. He is thinking of selling it off as a holiday home. No champagne, I'm afraid, but an excellent Chianti.'

He reached beneath the table for a carrier bag, producing the wine, glasses, crusty bread, cheese and olives, all carefully wrapped in tissue. 'And tomorrow we rise late, drive on to the *castello*—it is not far. It will be ready for us. Chiara has in-

structions to leave all the doors and windows wide
open to get rid of the smell of paint. But for tonight we have a large bed upstairs, with soft linen
and—'

'You're insane!' she yelled at him, in a flurry of
anguish. He expected her to share that bed, then
take off with him for more of the same back at his
cousin's castle? 'What's poor Helen going to think?
Or don't you give a damn? What's she doing?
Trying to have a lovely honeymoon all on her own?
Wondering when her new husband is going to turn
up and show an interest?

'And what about your cousin, Emilia? Won't she
mind your sneaking your bit on the side into her
home, dodging the workmen and painters and dec-
orators? The poor woman's trying to turn it into a
hotel, for pity's sake!' Beside herself, practically in
pieces, she howled, 'Or is she so used to your gross
behaviour she won't bat an eyelid?'

'Carissima!' He reached for her. The torment had
lasted long enough. But he'd had to be sure. And
now he was, humbly, gloriously sure.

Without quite knowing how, she was in his arms,
and his touch was so tender, so loving, she dissolved into helpless tears. And he rocked her,
holding her bright head against his chest until the
storm abated enough for her to hear his whispered,
'My lovely one, I'm sorry. So sorry. But it was
necessary. I had to know that the dreadful things
you said to me when I saw you last were said in
pain and self-defence and not in truth.'

He tucked a finger beneath her chin, his soft
silvery eyes searching her face. 'When you said
you'd never loved me, that you wanted me out of

your life, that you'd changed your mind about coming to me, I was angry enough to pull the building down around our heads with my bare hands.'

His thumb brushed her trembling lips. 'I'd spent long days and nights wondering if you'd choose the safety of marriage to Tom and your family's approval over living with me. I'd promised myself I'd put no pressure on you; it had to be your own decision. But the fact that you hadn't already given him his marching orders worried me. And I found I couldn't keep away. You'd told me you'd be seeing him on that Sunday and I had to follow. But I was so on edge I couldn't trust myself to speak to you without pleading my case, begging you—'

'Then Helen told you she was having your child,' she supplied with thick misery, burying her head back into his chest, taking this last little comfort. 'I understand why you felt you had to marry her.'

'Helen married Tom,' he said gently, stroking her tumbled hair. 'She is having his child. I have never made love to your sister.'

'Tom! She married Tom? But they hate each other! And you did. You told me you had!' She was incoherent. She couldn't take it in. Any of it. Except—except—Luca hadn't married Helen!

'What did I say, *carissima*? Tell me.' He cupped her face in his hands, gazing deeply into her huge green eyes. 'Why did you believe Helen and I had been lovers? I think I know, but tell me all the same.'

'Something you said.' She frowned, trying to remember. 'It was when I thought you were an item, and you said you had no intention of marrying again, unless—as it came out later—you wanted children. You said you'd met her at a party.' She bit on her lip. 'That she wanted backing for a new business and that—that these things happen.'

'Sweet idiot!' He dropped a kiss on her parted lips and desire flooded her with fierce delight. She clung to him but he held her slightly away, his face kinder, more compassionate than she'd ever seen it. 'I was speaking generally. People do exchange sex for financial favours, my little innocent. Only I'm not one of them.

'I don't like to bad-mouth your sister, *cara*, but the signals were all there. If I'd insisted, she would have obliged. But I would never operate that way. I looked over her business proposal and it was excellent. Helen and I have never been lovers.'

Still holding her hands, he led her to the table and sat her down on one of the chairs. Too bemused to do anything else, Bess watched him open the wine, cut the bread and the cheese, her eyes wide and fuddled because the world had turned itself upside down, revealing a paradise she hadn't known existed.

And he told her, 'When you told me you didn't want me any more I was burnt out with an emotion I'd never had before. It took me a while to realise what it was.' He poured a glass of wine and gently curved her fingers round the stem. 'Love. I was in love with you and it took a bombshell to make me realise it.' He sat beside her, cutting a tiny square of cheese and popping it into her mouth. Her eyes were huge with the magic of knowing . . .

'You love me?'

'With my life,' he answered solemnly. 'With hindsight, I think I fell in love with you the moment I saw you. And I knew you loved me. At least, I hope so.' He brushed her hair back off her face, his touch so tender that it made her want to cry. 'I couldn't believe that all you'd felt for me was lust. You'd been so responsive, so generous, so adorably loving.

'So during these last weeks I worked it all out,' he said, with the touch of arrogance she'd always found compelling. 'While you were seeing Tom, Helen broke down and confessed to what had happened. With the suddenness of a summer storm, she and Tom had discovered they were in love— love and hate—opposite sides of the same coin, *cara*. They hadn't been able to help themselves. Out of one of their violent arguments passion had sprung. And, as luck would have it, she immediately became pregnant.

'Poor old Tom didn't know how to tell you. But then he didn't have to, did he? You walked in and broke off the engagement. His relief must have sent him light-headed. The poor guy had been given a reprieve. He hadn't had to tell you—or any of the parents—of his naughty deeds! He and Helen were free to marry without anyone being able to accuse him of anything.

'But Helen didn't know that, of course. When you came back she naturally assumed Tom had told you all. When she'd phoned him to warn him you were there, and coming to see him, and he'd better see you at the office rather than at his home, it had been arranged that he'd tell you everything.

'She had no way of knowing you'd only gone to see him to tell him your engagement was off. So she let slip about the pregnancy—or maybe her conscience was really bothering her and she wanted to try to make you understand, not blame her too much. And you, characteristically, jumped to the conclusion that it was my child!'

He reached for her, pulling her onto his lap, tracing a fingertip down the side of her face, her neck. 'Having sorted all that out, I used undue pressure to make Mark tell me where you were and came to find out if my detective work proved me right. And it did. You couldn't hide your true feelings, no matter how you tried.

'And the *castello* is mine. I made Emilia an offer she couldn't refuse. It will be our Italian home. And, just to make sure you don't try to jump out of your pigeon-hole, we shall marry. I am going to bind you to me every way I can.'

'Luca...' she breathed deliriously, stroking the side of his lean and handsome face. 'I think I'm too stunned to take all this in.'

His wife. His love. For ever. She was too small to contain such happiness. The whole world was too small to contain it!

But she'd do her best!

'Don't worry about it, *carissima*,' he murmured against her mouth as his long hands caressed her body, scorching her flesh through the thin T-shirt. 'I will help you. All you have to do is love me.'

'Always,' she breathed ecstatically.

'Now?' His voice was suddenly thick, unsteady. Bright colour slashed his angular cheekbones. She found his lips and kissed them fiercely and he gathered her up, carrying her to the wooden staircase, the beat of his heart heavy beneath her cheek.

'Now,' she affirmed. 'Always, she promised.

She spared a very fleeting thought for her suitcases back in Rome. She had nothing with her. Not even a comb.

She didn't care.

This gorgeous, unforgettably wonderful love of her life was all she needed. Now and for ever.

# Take 4 bestselling love stories FREE

## Plus get a FREE surprise gift!

## Special Limited-time Offer

**Mail to Harlequin Reader Service®**

### 3010 Walden Avenue
### P.O. Box 1867
### Buffalo, N.Y. 14240-1867

**YES!** Please send me 4 free Harlequin Presents® novels and my free surprise gift. Then send me 6 brand-new novels every month, which I will receive months before they appear in bookstores. Bill me at the low price of $2.90 each plus 25¢ delivery and applicable sales tax, if any*. That's the complete price and a savings of over 10% off the cover prices—quite a bargain! I understand that accepting the books and gift places me under no obligation ever to buy any books. I can always return a shipment and cancel at any time. Even if I never buy another book from Harlequin, the 4 free books and the surprise gift are mine to keep forever.

106 BPA A3UL

| | | |
|---|---|---|
| Name | (PLEASE PRINT) | |
| Address | Apt. No. | |
| City | State | Zip |

This offer is limited to one order per household and not valid to present Harlequin Presents® subscribers. *Terms and prices are subject to change without notice. Sales tax applicable in N.Y.

UPRES-696                                                ©1990 Harlequin Enterprises Limited

**Coming in August 1997!**

# THE BETTY NEELS RUBY COLLECTION

August 1997—Stars Through the Mist

September 1997—The Doubtful Marriage

October 1997—The End of the Rainbow

November 1997—Three for a Wedding

December 1997—Roses for Christmas

January 1998—The Hasty Marriage

COLLECTOR'S EDITION

This August start assembling the
Betty Neels Ruby Collection. Six of the
most requested and best-loved titles have
been especially chosen for this collection.
From August 1997 until January 1998,
one title per month will be available to avid
fans. Spot the collection by the lush ruby red
cover with the gold Collector's Edition banner
and your favorite author's name—Betty Neels!

Available in August at your favorite retail outlet.

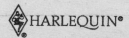

**HARLEQUIN®**

BNRUBY

# Free Gift Offer

With a Free Gift proof-of-purchase
from any Harlequin® book, you can receive
a beautiful cubic zirconia pendant.

This stunning marquise-shaped stone is a genuine cubic
zirconia—accented by an 18" gold tone necklace.
(Approximate retail value $19.95)

## Send for yours today...
## compliments of ⊕HARLEQUIN®

To receive your free gift, a cubic zirconia pendant, send us one original proof-of-purchase, photocopies not accepted, from the back of any Harlequin Romance®, Harlequin Presents®, Harlequin Temptation®, Harlequin Superromance®, Harlequin Intrigue®, Harlequin American Romance®, or Harlequin Historicals® title available at your favorite retail outlet, together with the Free Gift Certificate, plus a check or money order for $1.65 U.S./$2.15 CAN. (do not send cash) to cover postage and handling, payable to Harlequin Free Gift Offer. We will send you the specified gift. Allow 6 to 8 weeks for delivery. Offer good until December 31, 1997, or while quantities last. Offer valid in the U.S. and Canada only.

# Free Gift Certificate

Name: _____

Address: _____

City: _____ State/Province: _____ Zip/Postal Code: _____

Mail this certificate, one proof-of-purchase and a check or money order for postage and handling to: HARLEQUIN FREE GIFT OFFER 1997. In the U.S.: 3010 Walden Avenue, P.O. Box 9071, Buffalo NY 14269-9057. In Canada: P.O. Box 604, Fort Erie, Ontario L2Z 5X3.

## FREE GIFT OFFER                           084-KEZ

ONE PROOF-OF-PURCHASE
To collect your fabulous FREE GIFT, a cubic zirconia pendant, you must include this
original proof-of-purchase for each gift with the properly completed Free Gift Certificate.

Look what Santa brought!

# CHRISTMAS DELIVERY

Capture the holiday spirit with these three
heartwarming stories of moms, dads,
babies and mistletoe. *Christmas Delivery*
is the perfect stocking stuffer featuring three
of your favorite authors:

**A CHRISTMAS MARRIAGE** by Dallas Schulze
**DEAR SANTA** by Margaret St. George
**THREE WAIFS AND A DADDY** by Margot Dalton

There's always room for one more—
especially at Christmas!

Available wherever Harlequin and Silhouette
books are sold.

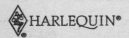